MOONSHINE

MOONSHINE

JUSTIN BENTON

CALKINS CREEK
An Imprint of Boyds Mills & Kane
New York

For information about permission to reproduce selections from this book,
please contact permissions@bmkbooks.com.

Calkins Creek
An Imprint of Boyds Mills & Kane
calkinscreekbooks.com
Printed in the United States of America

ISBN: 978-1-62979-811-0 (Hardcover)
ISBN: 978-1-68437-898-2 (eBook)
Book data is on file with the Library of Congress.

First edition
10 9 8 7 6 5 4 3 2 1

Design by Tim Gillner
The text is set in Bembo.
The titles are set in Bebas.

This book is dedicated to Julian and Mia.

MOONSHINE

CHAPTER

1

AUGUST 1, 1932

I **SWORE OFF DRINKING WHISKEY** the night before I turned thirteen. I made that decision while throwing up my first glass of moonshine out in the woods where Pa and I secretly made the stuff. It was a test of sorts between him and me, and I guess I flunked it.

It was just hours until my birthday, but Pa didn't think that was reason enough to miss a night's work. As usual, we headed into the woods at what he called the "witching hour." At that time of the evening, right when the lightning bugs showed up, I could feel a change in my blood. The night made me feel alive, and being nocturnal was of course a natural benefit for us moonshiners.

That night, I mixed the mash as we worked around the fire, circling the big copper pot like the hands on a pocket watch. Pa dumped a half sack of sugar into the cornmeal mash, and right as everything got to bubbling and boiling, I snugged the lid on top of the pot. Soon enough, all that steam off the mash would start shooting through the copper pipes, finally spiraling down the worm. The worm was a coil of pipe that looked like a giant spring and went down into the condenser barrel full of cold creek water. When that hot steam corkscrewed down the worm, the cold would shock it back into a liquid. It was like magic, though, because it wasn't just any liquid, it was our own brand of corn whiskey.

The wind skipped over the edge of the condenser barrel with a whistle. Through the smoke, I could see Pa staring into his clear glass of shine, thinking hard.

He looked across the pot at me. "It's your birthday now," he said.

I glanced up at the sky. The crescent moon sat lopsided over the tops of the pines. That meant it was around half past midnight.

"I figure it is."

"And I got a surprise for you, Cub," he said.

We had never been ones to over-celebrate a birthday, but we usually made do.

"A birthday present?"

Pa shook his head, his long gray hair swinging over his shoulders.

"I don't know you'd call it that exactly."

I stopped scraping off the mixing stick and looked at him. He was up to something.

"What do you mean, Pa?"

"I mean now that you're thirteen you've got to go to the schoolhouse. No more classes with Miss Avery."

I didn't go to school with the other kids. Never had. Miss Avery had been my teacher since I was four or five, giving me lessons right there in our cabin. She had been a teacher at some big school up in Virginia, probably about a hundred years ago, and Pa had gotten special permission for her to teach me at home a couple hours a week so I could be around to help him farm. Of course, farming for us meant brewing big potfuls of whiskey on the sly, but I was still getting an education.

Between Pa and Miss Avery, I had learned animals and sums and could even read a bit. The classes weren't overly long, and Pa only had to pay her a half-gallon a week for tuition. It had been a square deal for all of us. The fact was, though, that I'd always thought of my book learning as a temporary thing. I'd already mastered a trade.

"I don't need any more teaching, Pa. I always figured I'd be a shineman like you."

"You'd make a fine one, no denying that. But that government lady has been by twice now, and she says you've got to start this year. If you don't, she'll send the sheriff. You know we don't need the law coming around here."

Staring at the flames crawling up the copper still, I thought on this school business. Some mornings I'd catch sight of a group of students slinking off to classes all sleepy-eyed, looking sorry like a pack of beat dogs. Then in the afternoons they'd make their jailbreak and run out of that schoolhouse whooping like a bunch of savages. I was supposed to trade my days sleeping and nights under the stars for that? Whatever school was, I figured I'd been smart to avoid it so far.

Pa said, "It ain't so bad. And don't tell me you've never been curious about it."

I suppose I had been a little curious. More than that, I had wondered what the kids there were like. I spent my time with Pa or by myself mostly. Thinking about it, I realized those town kids probably had lots of experience with schooling, probably had it down cold. And I imagine they wouldn't exactly go out of their way to welcome an outsider.

Pa seemed to read my mind because he said, "And it's about time you met some folks your own age. I can't be raising a wild animal out here. You remember what happened with our pet coyote."

13

Just thinking about that coyote made me laugh, and I felt a bit better. Pa had brought that pup in to pull buckshot out of his hide when I was about eight. We had a fine time playing with him while he healed up. But once he was walking again, that thing went savage and tore the whole house to shreds. If Pa yelled at him, he would run into Pa's bedroom and pee right on the bed. I thought that was hilarious and a good sign of smarts too. That was until I tried to punish him and he did the same thing on my bed. A week later during a full moon, he howled once and jumped right out the kitchen window. We had not been sad to see him go.

"Quit your daydreaming, boy. Help me get the fire going hot again."

I started feeding the fire, but in my head, I kept imagining a class full of students and some fancy professor laughing as I bumbled my way through a lesson. Before I realized it, I'd pitched about a dozen trees' worth of deadwood under the pot. I was standing close enough to catch my overalls on fire, but all I felt was an ice chunk in my stomach.

"Pa, we've just got too much work for me to go off to school."

I rushed over to rinse all the glasses in the rainwater barrel so he could see how busy I was helping him shine. How was Pa going to get by without me?

"And don't kids go to school an awful lot?" I asked. "It's every Monday and Thursday, isn't it?"

Pa bit his lip and gave me a worried look.

"Uh, it's a little more than that. But you've still got three weeks of summer. And you'll do all right. I promise."

The fire was crackling good, and as I passed it an ember popped up onto my overalls. Brushing at it, I took a step back and almost knocked Pa's jar of moonshine off the top of the condenser barrel. I grabbed it and leaned against the still, staring hard into the glass like I'd always seen Pa do when he was thinking.

Pa squatted down, his knee bones popping like twigs, and he flicked at the drip tube as the shine trickled out. He looked up and saw me holding his glass.

"No need to drown your sorrows about school," he said with a grin.

I kind of smiled and started to hand him his glass, but then stopped. That whiskey was still in my hand. I had spent nearly every night of my life back here in the woods making the stuff for folks to drink. I should at least be able to try it. Then maybe Pa would see I was man enough not to be bothered with school.

I lifted Pa's moonshine up to have a little sip, but before I could even put my mouth to the glass, the fumes off the stuff punched me square in the nose. My whole head nearly jumped backwards off my shoulders like I'd smelled an old dead mouse.

Pa shook his head but kept smiling at me. He wasn't going to stop me from drinking it. He was waiting for me to stop myself.

"That's a good batch to try, boy, our secret flavor too. Finest in Tennessee. And it tastes even better than it smells," he said with a laugh.

That first sip, that first little bit I got past my lips, I swear it scorched a hole straight through my tongue. My eyes watered up, and I couldn't make that whiskey go anywhere. It was just sitting there like I was holding a fireball in my mouth.

"Are you going to swallow it, or you just savoring it?" he asked.

If he'd kept his mouth shut I probably would have spit that moonshine right on the ground. But he was just so tickled by it that it was like he was daring me, so I choked it down like I was swallowing a baseball. My stomach bucked, but I kept it down.

"Aren't you going to tell me how good we made it? Or you ain't man enough yet to appreciate it?" Pa asked. He was having himself a big time now.

I didn't say anything—just gave him the meanest look I could muster, then took an even bigger gulp to show him I could handle myself.

"Uh-oh," he said.

I was drunk right off. And it wasn't what I'd call fun. The feeling reminded me of when I was a little fella and I'd turn circles in the yard, just whirling around until I'd spun myself stupid. The only thing I could focus on was the moon overhead, and I took a notion to howl at it, but my guts clenched up. Next thing I knew, that whiskey was coming right back up into the sticker bushes.

I kept heaving that shine out of me and decided then and there that my drinking days were done. I tried to stand straight but was just twisting around like a leaf in the breeze. Pa came running and grabbed me right before I hit the ground.

The squawking of hens in the coop out back woke me the next morning. For a second I was surprised to find myself in my own bed. The memory of having drunk moonshine came back to me, followed shortly by the recollection I had to start school. Thirteen was shaping up to be a heck of a year.

I was getting dressed when I heard a rumbling coming down our drive. I walked out to the kitchen and saw Pa standing by the table, looking as startled as I was. The only visitors we ever had were during a sale, and none of those folks had the money for an automobile. Pa stepped fast out the door, his long legs crossing our whole house in two steps. I ran over to the window to peek out.

The county sheriff's Model A was parked out front. Sheriff Bardo was climbing out, looking at our little cabin and frowning about as hard as I'd ever seen a person frown. The sheriff did a good job of making himself look like an Old West lawman out of one of the motion pictures, with his silver mustache and that giant white cowboy hat he wore.

My first thought was he'd found the still in the woods, but there'd been no sign last night of anyone else having been out there. I stood there panicking, then remembered that government lady. Maybe she'd called the sheriff early about my going to school. If that was it, then I owed it to Pa to make sure he didn't get in trouble on account of me. I ran out onto the porch to join him.

Pa met him in front of his patrol car, and the sheriff said, "Earl Jennings, you make me search those woods and I'm going to be real unhappy. You and I both know you've been making liquor."

"Liquor?" Pa said, his face all scrunched up like he was confused. "No, sir. That's against the law."

The sheriff passed a fat wad of chewing tobacco from one cheek to the other, his meaty face puffed up on one side. I slunk up next to Pa.

"You moonshine too, boy?" the sheriff asked. He looked me up and down.

I opened my mouth to say something but couldn't, so I just focused on my boots and kept quiet. This was worse than any business about school.

I watched the sheriff's shadow cover my boots as he leaned in over me. He made a horrible swishing noise, then let fly a soupy brown gob of tobacco spit that splashed down next to me. I stared at it, scared to look up.

"You're that boy who doesn't go to school, aren't you?" he said.

I shuffled around there in the dust, waiting for Pa to say something for me.

The sheriff laughed and said, "You ain't even teach him to talk, Earl?"

"You got the wrong men," Pa said. "We aren't doing anything wrong."

"You're no different from any other crook here in Hidden

Orchard. And don't tell me you've never heard of Prohibition. Congress passed that law more than ten years ago, so anybody who makes, sells, or drinks alcohol is a criminal. You stop making moonshine, or I'll take you to jail for as long as I want."

The word *jail* hit me so hard I thought my heart had stopped.

"You can't do that," I stammered.

I looked at Pa to be sure, but he didn't look back at me. He was staring right through the sheriff, like he was about to tear into him.

The sheriff leaned down toward me and said, "So you can talk? Well, you be a good little boy and wait your turn because this is grown-up business. If you wanna say something, say so long to your pa."

"Get out of here," Pa growled. I saw his hands curl into fists by his sides.

The sheriff only smiled under his big hat.

"Go ahead, Earl. Take a swing. See what I do to you. Last deadbeat who tried to test me is rotting in jail now."

For a long moment, nobody moved or spoke. I'd seen Pa brawl a few times before, mostly attacked by customers and once by bandits. I had never seen him beat, though I prayed nights I never saw him fight again. Anything that hurt him, hurt me. Pa finally took a step back and put a hand on my shoulder.

"No more shining," the sheriff said again as he backed toward the police car. "I looked the other way on your piddling little operation out of pity for you and this boy. And because I'm such a charitable man, I'll even let you get rid of what you've got. But you best find a new trade. Prohibition, Earl. You make alcohol, you go to jail."

The sheriff gave me an awful smile and then took off in his automobile.

Pa asked, "You all right?"

"Is he serious, Pa? He knows we've been shining. He said he was going to search the woods."

My insides were juddering like a jar of jelly. I couldn't take my eyes off the dust cloud at the end of the drive.

"He won't find a thing."

Pa wiped his face with his sleeve and headed back in. I kept standing there feeling stuck in the mud, wondering how I was going to keep Pa out of jail if I was trapped in the schoolhouse all day.

CHAPTER

2

TWO **WEEKS PASSED** with no further sign of the sheriff, but not one minute went by without me worrying about jails. We didn't stop shining though, not even for one night. Pa made a big point of saying it was a bluff, maybe a call for a bribe. He even said if the sheriff weren't a lawman, he'd sock him right in his fat melon for how he'd talked to me. Still I sensed that something big was on the horizon, like before a tornado, when my bones felt electric and the air smelled hot.

That morning, the sun had barely risen when a nightmare of Sheriff Bardo creeping through our woods and grabbing me spooked me awake. I couldn't get back to sleep, so finally I just got up and pulled my red blanket up across my old horsehair mattress. My room was easy to keep straight because there was hardly anything in it—my mattress, and on the floor, two drawers from a dresser for keeping my shirts. Pa had the other two drawers in his room. Neither one of us had the actual dresser.

The kitchen was empty, so I pulled the black pan off the wall and sawed off some chunks of ham to throw in. When the fat was bubbling around the ham and the pan was good and greased up, I cracked a pair of eggs into it. I'd been making breakfast for myself for four years now, usually for Pa as well.

The back door clapped and Pa came stomping through in his boots and faded coveralls. His hands were so dirty it looked like he'd been soaking them in oil. There was no telling what time he'd gotten up to work around the farm, or if he'd even gone to bed at all.

"Eat up! Get your energies up. We got work to do," he said.

He was a mess of energy no matter what time of day.

"You eat, Pa?"

"Yeah, but that don't mean I can't do it again."

Pa slid into a chair at our wobbly two-man table, and I dumped some ham and eggs onto our tin plates. The salty smell filled our little cabin and would hang around until a wind pushed it through the cracks in the old wood panels.

"Pa, how long I got 'til school starts?"

He patted my shoulder. "You sure are worked up over schooling."

"I can't help it."

"A couple days. And I won't lie to you. School can be downright awful. There are times it will crush your whole spirit. But it can also be good—real good. Because it gives you opportunities."

"Opportunities, Pa?"

"Take me, for example. A schooled man," he said, puffing his chest out. "Now my old neighbor Otis did not go to school. So I had lots of opportunities to tell him he was stupid."

I chuckled and got up to scrape our plates. That day Pa had an old corn sheller that needed fixing and likely a good cussing, so I left him to it. Pa had a way with mechanics and fixing things like I couldn't believe and which, sadly, he had not passed on to me. One time the whole engine block on the hospital's ambulance seized up and not one of their experts could fix it. Pa went up there with a roll of baling wire and a horseshoer's hand file and had that thing running in a half hour. My chores around the house were more focused on our food, so I headed out the back door to check on the garden.

Pa had set up the little side garden years ago, back when it was just tomatoes and cucumbers. Each spring we'd add one new thing, like sweet potatoes, squash, or peas, and then that fall we'd have something new. That was the idea at least, but one year the jackrabbits came in and nearly wiped us out. The next year it was the snails, and if it wasn't them, it was the gophers.

We were getting attacked from all sides and had to bring out the big guns if we wanted to eat. And we did that by doing something so fool-headed I still can't believe it worked. We junked up the garden. I quit weeding for two weeks. We threw table scraps and bread crumbs and chicken feed and an old tire right there by the peas. Mice showed up by the dozens. And the old jackrabbits and snails and gophers were in heaven. They were eating us out of house and home. Until the snakes came.

From the porch, Pa and I once counted three black snakes zipping along the vegetable rows and just feasting. I put an old tin pan full of creek water for them out by the tomatoes, and as long as we kept that tire there as a hiding-hole, we could always count on at least one snake standing watch over our garden.

That day, I just weeded a little bit, careful not to spook any of the snakes, then cut across the north end of the cornfield and made my way to a cleared-out patch at the edge of the woods. It was my thinking place for when something was pressing down on me.

Ma's gravestone still had some old dried bluebonnet flowers wedged against it. I walked the half-circle around it, careful not to step directly in front of the marker, and sat down in the canary grass. The way her grave was angled and how I was sitting, it was like we were both looking out past the corn at the house. The midday sun was burning down on its tin roof and making it shine like silver.

"I start school in a few days," I said out loud. "And I'm thirteen now, but I guess you know that."

A fat grasshopper fluttered out of the clover and up past my face. I didn't move, just rested back on my elbows and breathed in the breeze.

"And I think me and Pa are about to get in a lot of trouble. I can't tell if he even sees it coming. I'd fix it if I could, but I don't know how. Maybe I'll learn how in school. I don't know."

I got up and nodded to the grass and headed back home. If Ma were still around, I bet she'd sort this whole mess out, and we wouldn't have to worry about nothing. If she thought Pa was acting foolish, I bet she'd tell him so and he'd say, "You're right, dear," and everything would be settled.

I wanted to tell him my worries about this business with the sheriff, but it wasn't my place. We were a team. Questioning him on family matters was heading into traitor territory, and besides, if I couldn't trust him, who was left? Me?

That afternoon before work, we headed down the path and had just reached the shade of the big oak when Pa stopped. He turned to me with this real clever grin and said, "I've got a surprise for you."

His last surprise had been me going to school. I kicked at the dirt and said, "I ain't exactly sure I want any surprises."

"This is more like a real good secret."

"What's the secret?"

He shook his head and smiled like we were playing a game.

"Where we at?" he asked.

23

I shrugged. "The tree, Pa, but that ain't a secret. I've been up it a hundred times."

"We ain't going up."

He kept on grinning at me and waiting for me to figure out his riddle. We were on the path to the clearing, right under the big oak. I looked around the rest of the woods, but things looked about the same as they had yesterday, and the thousand yesterdays before that. We were right next to the tree, so I figured it held the secret.

The tree towered over everything else on our land, but it wasn't just its tallness that made this particular oak "the tree" in a forest full of hickory, spruce, and pine. Its bottom branches angled downwards and ricocheted off the thick brush, making the trunk look like it had sprouted spider legs. If five men were to try to wrap their hands around the trunk in a ring, they wouldn't reach.

I kept studying the tree, and all of a sudden Pa turned and left the trail. I followed him around to the back side of the oak, where there was nothing but bright-red briars all tangled up on the ground. This side never got much sun and smelled like wet wood and rot year-round. Pa picked up a stick and shoved the end of it under the curtain of thorns. He levered it up and made a space between the dirt and the briars.

"Go on under. See what you can see."

"I ain't going under there, Pa. Ain't nothing to see and nothing to do but get cut up."

"Hurry up and get going. If you're not fast enough, all these thorns are going to come down on your head. I'll be right behind you."

I groaned and dropped down to my stomach and peered into the darkness. Army-crawling on my knees and elbows, I inched forward. The earth felt smooth under my palms, and I realized someone had been down there before. I hooked my pants on thorns twice but kept crawling. The tunnel finally blossomed out and I saw there was space to stand under a canopy of briars and yellow leaves.

Pa called from the other side, "You up?"

Looking around, I started to grin. The sunlight barely trickled in through the ceiling of sticker bushes, but I could see that the briars formed a little room next to the oak. Pa slithered in next to me seconds later.

"It's like a cocoon, Pa," I said.

He reached into a dark crack in the oak's trunk. His hand came back out cradling a copper bowl with a half-melted white candle in it.

"You keep that here, Pa?" I asked.

With a funny grin he said, "I keep a lot of things back here."

He flipped a match against the back of his two front teeth and the flame ignited with a hiss right in front of his face. With the candle lit, Pa stooped down to squeeze himself through the hole in the oak.

"Wait, Pa," I said.

"It's all right, son," he said, his voice echoing deep from inside the oak.

I wiggled through the crack and followed him into what felt like a giant wooden cave inside the tree. Something in there smelled mighty familiar. As Pa lit row after row of white candles in lantern glasses, my eyes adjusted, and I saw, among other things, a stockpile of moonshine that could take down an army. The insides of the oak trunk had been fitted with rickety boards that made for shelves holding all different shapes and sizes of green and purple bottles.

I turned a full circle, admiring the size of the wooden room and the different levels of glasses. It was like a spiral staircase of shelves, with the big jars and fat oak barrels sitting low, while all the fine glass bottles twisted up nearly out of sight. With a dozen candles lit, the yellow light bounced from jar to jar and the tree glowed warm.

"So what do you think?" Pa asked.

I couldn't get over how danged pretty and put together the whole thing looked. There were even footholds cut into one side of the room, likely for climbing up and reaching the highest shelves.

"But who made this?" I asked.

"Me, of course," he said, beaming.

I should have known. Only Pa could have turned an old tree into a work of art.

"Told you it was a surprise," he said.

It was a bombshell all right.

"Why didn't you tell me about this before?" I asked. "You think I'd get us caught?"

"Nothing like that. This is more for an emergency. Or for you if something happened to me."

That was an ugly thought, about the ugliest possible. Was he talking like if he went to jail? Or did he mean something worse?

"But when did you put everything in here?" I asked.

"Early mornings I'd barrel an extra batch or two. Roll it on through the briars and cut myself to bits. Just little times when I could."

I let all this sink in. It was a lot to take. How had I never figured it out?

"You got any more secrets?" I asked. I reckoned I didn't know Pa as well as I thought I did.

"Yes, sir. I am terrified of spiders and I prefer not to be in the company of ducks. But other than that, you know it all now."

I let my eyes wander up the different levels of bottles again. The place *was* beautiful. And if I hadn't come up on it in twelve years of running through the woods, I doubted the sheriff could find it.

"I reckon we're full-on partners now," Pa said as he snuffed out the candles. "And tomorrow we're going to see an old associate of mine. Our first proper meeting as partners."

I couldn't help but smile. Partners. That was the real surprise. It looked like I'd become a full-on shineman earlier than I'd planned. I felt the thrill of something new in my stomach, but it was not all gladness like I would have expected.

The more I thought on it, I realized this was a heck of a time to get promoted, what with the sheriff saying he was going to bust us. If we were partners, did that mean we'd go to the same jail if they busted us? I wriggled out of the brambles and stood with scratched-up elbows and what felt like the whole world on my shoulders.

Pa started off down the trail, and I ran to catch up to him.

"Did you show me the tree now because I turned thirteen or because the sheriff came?"

He smiled his one-sided grin at me and announced to the woods, "Write it down in the history books—at age thirteen, Cub Jennings officially became smarter than his old man."

I laughed as we walked on, but didn't correct him.

"What's the meeting about, Pa?"

"To see how we can get the sheriff off our backs. That way you won't have to worry about it the next day."

"What's the next day?"

"School. Day one."

CHAPTER 3

WE SET OUT FOR THE BIG MEETING noontime the
next day, and right before we hit the end of our dusty drive, I asked
Pa why we shined. Shining had always come as natural to me as
walking or talking, but now with the sheriff's threat of jail, I was
feeling like I didn't have a right idea of it.

He kept walking, never falling out of step, but I could see the
plainness of my question had caught him by surprise.

"You don't like it?" he asked.

"Of course I do, Pa. I just never really thought about why we
do it. Now I have."

We rounded the corner of our east field and headed down the
side of the main road into town, Pa silent. I knew he was thinking
though, because he was bobbing his head like a chicken.

"I reckon you mean why don't we just farm? Am I right?" he
asked, motioning to our field.

That was kind of what I'd meant, so I nodded.

"It's a fair question, son. Especially since making shine ain't exactly legal."

"I know, Pa, and I won't tell nobody," I swore. "Never have, never will."

"I know you won't tell. And we don't need a fancy life, but with our tiny patch of crops, selling corn is only going to bring us misery and rock soup."

We both looked over at our field, at the dried-out stalks that didn't even come up to my shoulders. As far as a farm went, we certainly weren't going to be winning any prizes. I'd seen some farms—plantations, they called them—that were bigger than a whole town. We had twenty-two acres of corn so ugly the crows didn't even come.

Pa went on. "But imagine we take the little bit of corn we do grow and turn it into something that sells for more money. Let's say we take that same bushel, run it through the furnace here, and then sell the Old Jennings white lightning for a quarter a jar. We do that every two weeks, and you know how much money we got then?"

He was walking faster now, excited.

"How much, Pa?"

"A heck of a lot more than we'd get for corn, that's how much."

"But it's against the law," I said.

Something about that first drink—in fact everything about it—had me thinking maybe there was a good reason this stuff was illegal. And the sheriff sure enough felt the same way.

Pa sighed, and I could tell he wanted to help me understand but didn't know how. We walked on past the Jefferson place, where an old, hunched-over woman was dragging a burlap picking sack down the rows of cotton. The bolls had barely started to peek white, and I knew she wouldn't fetch a good price for early cotton. Surely she knew it too, which meant she must have been real hard up to be picking now. Off in the distance, I could make out the steeple of Beckwith Methodist. We didn't live but three miles out of town, but sometimes it felt twice that.

Finally, Pa said, "Lemme ask you something. You remember when your ma passed away?"

I shook my head. I'd tried plenty of times, but I never could really remember it.

"You weren't but a young pup then. But when she went, some folks around here wanted to take you off to Nashville. Said I couldn't raise you on my own, us being a forty-year-old man and a boy and some half-dead crops."

"Nashville? I ain't got no business in Nashville."

"It was to put you in a place for boys whose families couldn't take care of 'em. Like an orphanage. The government folk can just snatch a boy up if they think he's underfed. And they were eyeing you. Of course I would've kicked and scratched like the devil if they'd tried it, but I found another way."

"Moonshining?"

Pa slowed his stride and laid a hand on my shoulder.

"I had a month to get you fed and looking right to pass their inspection. And when that government lady came back, you were sparkling like a new Ford. I told her your ma's family had inherited me some money. Told her money wasn't a concern anymore."

"So you lied to 'em."

"Dang it, boy. Yes, I lied to 'em. But you've got to understand why. I had to make a decision to work on the other side of the law. It was a hard decision, but it wasn't a decision at all, you know what I mean?"

We walked on, and I fell into a daze thinking about what Pa had said. He'd had to start shining because of me.

"It doesn't hurt no one, does it, Pa? I mean really hurt 'em?"

30

"There's more than one way of looking at things generally. Like a fire will keep you warm, but it'll burn you if you get too close. Or the oil lamp will help you see the way home, or it'll blind you if it's right in your eyes. I try to look at shining like that."

I nodded to him. "It's like we shine to get by, not just to do something bad. That's not hurting anybody."

He chuckled and said, "It'll blow you sky-high if it touches flame. Liquid dynamite. And of course it'll hurt your mouth if you drink too much."

Just the thought of drinking it made my whole body shudder. We had crafted this special flavor that customers were going goofy over, but I'll be danged if it hadn't tasted like sucking on a bonfire to me.

"It is against the law," Pa said. "No two ways about it. Even before Prohibition, making your own drink was illegal 'cause the government didn't get any money off it."

"But why should they get any money? They didn't make it."

Pa smiled at me real big like I'd pleased him, but I couldn't see why. I hadn't said anything that weren't real obvious.

"That's how most folks feel. But now you can't even take a drink of whiskey, much less make it. It's like it's double illegal."

I kicked a rock straight down the road and grinned at him. "Then I guess we've got to be double careful."

"We good then?" Pa asked, smiling back.

"Always, Pa."

We hit Main Street and I got those same funny jitters I felt whenever I went to town. It was the strangest thing—half of me always wanted to run back to the house and woods, but the other half kind of got a kick out of seeing all the people and fancy things.

I got a look into Gibbons Drugstore with its front window jammed with advertisements for candies and makeup powders and

Coca-Cola. A freckly boy inside the store looked out at me, and I wondered if he would be at the school. We stared at each other through the glass for a long second before Pa tugged me along.

The sidewalk was packed with the church crowd spilling out of Beckwith Methodist. A few of them gave Pa a less-than-friendly look. I didn't know if it was on account of his long hair or rumors of his occupation, but I pretended I didn't notice.

As we came up the big hill on Elm Street, I heard the *clop-clop* of a horse approaching.

The sheriff occasionally made his rounds on horseback, and I was scared he'd spotted us.

Pa nudged my elbow.

"You see that?" he asked, with a laugh.

I craned my neck and looked down the road toward the center of town. It was not the sheriff, but a rugged old mare pulling some kind of cart. A couple steps later, that gray horse and its load came into view and I started laughing as well. The cart had chrome fenders, a sleek black paint job, and an embarrassed-looking fellow sitting inside with his wrists perched on top of the steering wheel.

"It's an automobile, Pa."

"You remember Miss Avery telling you about President Hoover? There goes a Hoover carriage."

"But why's the horse pulling it?"

"No money for gasoline. Poor fella probably bought it a few years ago, lost his job or something. Happens more than you'd think."

I waved to the man and horse as they lumbered by and the man returned my greeting with a honk of the horn.

We turned left off Elm onto a dusty yellow road, and a shabby old mansion appeared in the distance. Purple wisteria climbed all over its walls and porch columns, its windows covered in a maze of dark vines.

"You been by here?" Pa asked.

"It looks haunted," I told him. It was plain to see.

This was not the kind of place I wanted to have my first big meeting, and if I had my choice I'd stay clear altogether, but Pa kept on, so I followed him into the yard. The grass was littered with piles of rusted machinery, an old harrow, some teeth off a plow. We finally reached a big front door sitting crooked on its hinges.

Pa said, "This fellow travels across the whole state for his business and he knows everything that happens, legal and illegal. He's safe to talk to. You ready?"

I took a deep breath.

"Always, Pa."

CHAPTER

4

Pa **KNOCKED AND THE LACE CURTAIN** covering the little window next to the door flew open. Two milky gray eyes peeked out. The door shot open, almost hitting Pa in the face, and an ancient man in shirtsleeves and a stiff black hat popped out.

"Well, hello!" he cried, throwing his hands up in a big show.

I watched in horror as the old man slowly peeled off his black hat. I half expected spiders to come running out.

"Hello, Herbert," Pa said. "This is my boy. You probably haven't seen him in ten years."

The man turned and stared at me, his smile pushing his powdery cheeks all the way up into his eyes.

"Young Cub. Last time I saw you, you were but a tot in your mother's arms. How do you do?"

"Hi," I mumbled. That was all I could manage there face-to-face with the skeleton.

"Cub, this is Mr. Herbert Yunsen," Pa said. "We used to work together."

The man appeared to be fishing around for something in the

34

side pocket of his black suit. His chalky hand came out with a rainbow of unwrapped sweets stuck to his palm. He extended the clump out to me in offering. Manners obliged me to peel off two candies like scabs.

The old man ushered us into what looked to have once been a fancy mansion, almost like a castle. We sat at a dining room table as long as a train car and I took a look around the room. Old portraits of unsmiling men and angry-looking women covered the walls, but apart from a wood-burning stove in the corner, the room felt almost empty. A draft blew in from above and my sweaty town shirt gave me a chill.

"So how's business, Herbert?" Pa asked, leaning back in his chair and smiling big. Pa was odd like that. You take him just about anywhere, and he'd set up shop so comfortable you'd think he'd been born there.

"Oh, just booming. More people dying every day," Mr. Yunsen replied, looking satisfied with himself.

So he's a killer, I thought.

Mr. Yunsen must've caught me looking at him funny because he leaned across the table and said, "Perhaps I should explain myself. I am a kind of doctor. A mortician. I prepare bodies for their final resting place."

This meeting was worse than I could have imagined.

Mr. Yunsen asked, "Are you also in the moonshine business, Cub?"

I was suddenly unsure of how much I wanted to be involved with all this. I couldn't get a solid *yes* to come out until I felt Pa's boot kicking at my shin under the table.

"Yes, sir."

"I was as well, once upon a time," Mr. Yunsen said, "though I focused more on the delivery side. Bootlegging, it's called. The transport of illegal goods, often at very high speeds."

"You ever think of running shine again?" Pa asked, leaning in, eyes wide with excitement.

"Think about it every time I get behind the wheel. You should see the Buick I've got . . ." He began to smile and his sentence trailed off. "But *think* about it is all I do. Those days are long gone for me. Now, I understand you gentlemen are concerned about the shine trade?"

I said, "More than concerned, sir."

"And rightly so, I fear. I've heard whispers that the shine business, and I don't know if this applies yet to Hidden Orchard, but in the rest of Tennessee the shine business is being consolidated into a single group."

"You mean folks are organizing?" Pa asked.

"No. An outside interest is taking over. A group from up North, I believe. Taking over private producers like yourselves. Consolidating and putting those private producers to work for them. Or eliminating them. Usually assisted by the local police force."

"But why would they come down here? We don't bother anybody," Pa said.

"It's no coincidence that a good bit of the country's liquor comes from this area. We have generations of knowledge and the room to grow. You don't believe someone's going to plant an acre of corn in New York City, do you? Or produce a single gallon without blowing themselves up?"

"So that's why the sheriff is after us now," Pa said. "Consolidating or eliminating."

"Sheriff Bardo?" Mr. Yunsen asked. His white eyebrows arched upwards and he shook his head. "As I understand it, people can be made to do most anything for the right amount of money."

I couldn't figure how a sheriff could be working with a group of shiners. Or whatever that group was from up North. So shiners either had to work for them, or they got eliminated. I knew which group we were in. At that moment, a figure passed through the doorway at the far end of the room, and I started, thinking maybe there really were ghosts there.

"Rebecca," Mr. Yunsen called. His voice echoed through the giant room. "Come say hello to some friends of mine."

The figure backed up into the doorframe and walked slowly toward us. It was a girl, wearing a faded gray dress with small purple flowers. She walked up on us real careful, studying us with eyes so big they looked like two walnuts. Her hair had sun streaks in it, proof of a summer spent outside.

"This is Rebecca, my granddaughter. Rebecca, this is Mr. Jennings and his son, Cub."

Me and the girl looked at each other cautiously. Pa stood up like a gentleman to greet her. She bowed slightly.

"Hello, dear," Pa said. "Are you starting school tomorrow?"

Her face turned grim and she nodded.

"You wouldn't happen to be in Miss Pounder's class, would you?" he asked.

She nodded again, lips pressed together tightly.

"What do you know, Cub is in Miss Pounder's class too."

My teacher was named Miss Pounder? That was not a good sign.

Rebecca turned and studied me hard. Turning back to Pa, she shook her head.

"You're wrong, mister. He's not at Hidden Orchard School. I've never seen him before."

"He has never gone to school before. Tomorrow will be his very first day," Pa said.

"He's never gone to school?" she asked. "Never ever?"

Pa shook his head. She looked at him with suspicious eyes. Then she turned to me, smiled about as warmly as I ever saw, and eased closer like she was approaching a scared puppy.

37

"Hi. My name is Re-bec-ca," she said slowly, tapping herself on the chest in time with the syllables. "Re-bec-ca."

"I know," I said. "Your grandpa just said so."

Even with her summer tan, her face turned bright red. Still though, she couldn't have been half as embarrassed as I was.

She muttered, "Oh, forgive me. I thought if you never went to school you were . . . you know . . . slow."

I felt myself flush too, but finally had to laugh a bit as well. "I've never been in school. But I can talk and stuff."

She smiled at me and mouthed the word *sorry*.

I relaxed a little and said, "Did you know that school is actually five days a week? It's Monday to Friday."

Pa had been prepping me on all the details.

Her mouth opened to respond, but no words came out for a long moment.

"You sure you're not slow?" she said.

"Pretty sure, yes."

She giggled and said, "Folks are going to eat you alive at school."

Before I could respond, Rebecca curtseyed to Pa and left.

Pa and Mr. Yunsen talked a little more, but my mind was distracted. I had met the first of my new schoolmates, and after ten seconds, she had determined I was somewhat of a dolt. After a few minutes, Mr. Yunsen led us out and shook our hands.

As we walked out into the sun, Pa said, "We got a big problem."

I stuck my hands in my pockets and said, "Yeah, at school tomorrow, people are going to think I'm some half-wit monkey."

"People are messing with the moonshine business."

He was right. There were two problems. I looked over at him and realized that one of those battles I was going to have to fight on my own.

CHAPTER

5

THE NEXT MORNING, around the time I normally would have been coming back from the still, I was heading for school, all dressed up in Pa's old church shirt he had made me put on, and my hair combed over to make me look a right fool. I was clutching my lunch bag so tight my fingers punched through the paper with a loud rip, dumping my biscuit and sausage onto the grass. I picked them up and blew as much dirt off as I could, then wrapped the food back up in the ragged paper and shoved the whole greasy mess into my pocket.

I reached Hidden Orchard and there was none of that little thrill I felt when I went there with Pa. Everyone was walking fast, heads down, all business. I had never been one to venture out into town just for the heck of it, though Pa would have let me if I'd asked. It had always seemed too big, and now it felt like it had grown two sizes overnight. All the sparkle was gone from it, and I knew the worst was yet to come.

As I came up on the stubby little school building, the chatter of folks my age snapped me out of my thoughts. A group of four girls wearing rough dresses sewn from flour sacks got real quiet when I walked by, then busted out laughing and squeaking. I took one last breath of free air and pushed through the schoolhouse door.

The whole building felt like it had been waiting for me. Pa had told me that this school was one of the nicest in the county, in that it had not just one room, but two. Everybody from ten to fourteen would have class in one room, and the older folks were in the other. There was a little hallway that was like a mineshaft, and I stood there looking for where to go as people pushed past me in big groups. Pa had told me all I had to do was find the right room, walk in, and sit down at one of the desks, taking care it was not the biggest one. That one was for the teacher. A sign in big black letters was tacked to the door on the right-hand side: POUNDER.

I walked in with my head down, didn't look at a soul, and dropped into a seat on the side of the room. A couple students were whispering to each other, and a big mountain of a lady with a red mouth stood up front. She was next to the big desk, and I was mighty glad I hadn't taken her spot. She had her white hair combed straight down from the middle of her head, and it hung down hard, making her look like an angry white gumdrop.

As more and more students filed in, I pressed my hands hard between my knees and looked around. There was a little patch of chalkboard behind the big woman. There were twelve oak desks, all different sizes, most with deep grooves and carvings in them. A flag drooped over the middle of the chalkboard, and there was a yellowed map of somewhere tacked onto the wall, a top corner loose and sagging.

The chairs were even worse than what we had at home. They were round pine logs, stumps barely big enough to hold a body, with a scrap of board nailed on the back of the log and sticking up to make a seat back. Some of the students were sneaking glances at me and whispering. The one thing I could be sure of in there was that I was the only new student.

As the last folks came running in, the woman at the front wrote something on the board, crashing the chalk into the board with each letter, like she was carving a gravestone.

"POUNDER. Arithmetic, Composition, and Social Graces."

There were six boys, including me, and six girls, not including the teacher. The kids looked how most kids looked, which was mostly normal with a couple exceptions. Rebecca was up at the front of the class. It felt like she was the only one who wasn't staring at me.

The teacher kept banging the chalk into the board, throwing up a cloud of white dust all around her.

Finally she turned and asked in a real deep voice, "Now who can read this for me?"

The buzz around the room stopped right there and everybody froze but me. I kept looking at the teacher and her eyes locked right on to mine.

"You, with the blond hair that needs cutting. Are you that new boy?" Her voice shook the whole room.

I could feel my head and my hair that needed cutting turtling into my shoulders.

"Um, yes."

She looked all insulted by my answer and tapped her foot like she was waiting for me to continue.

"Complete sentences in here, sir. Yes, what? 'Yes, you are.'"

"Um, okay, right. Yes, yes I are."

One of the flour sack girls next to me giggled, and then the rest of the class started cracking up. Their laughter was a punch in the gut, and the temperature in the room seemed to spike hot enough to light the schoolhouse on fire. I thought, I hate this place.

Miss Pounder said, "That is neither correct nor funny, if that was your aim. Now, who here can read this?"

Suddenly, everyone wanted to participate, and a bunch of hands shot up. A barefoot boy on the other side of the room read the words, and Miss Pounder took off on a string of announcements and exercises that finally drew the students' attention off of me.

It was a nightmare of a morning. In a moment of inspiration, I reached down onto my stump seat and picked off a thick splinter, then jabbed it into the web between my thumb and forefinger to see if it would wake me up. It was not a success, and I had to suffer through the spelling lesson with a bloody hand.

At lunch I sat by myself, eating my cold biscuit in the shade of a maple tree. A couple of boys with smudged faces ran around the yard with sticks, and a group of girls was singing and clapping out a song. Apart from Miss Pounder, I hadn't said a word to anybody all day, but I felt about as obvious as a fly in a pitcher of milk.

Something rustled behind the tree, and I guarded my biscuit between my knees. A voice called out from behind me, "Hi, Cub."

Rebecca Yunsen ran out from behind the tree and stood in front of me. She had on the same dress as the day before.

"Good job with Miss Pounder this morning. You're going to fit right in here."

"You think?"

"Sure. Almost everybody in our class is dumb."

"That's . . . good?"

She arched her eyebrows at me.

"How come you didn't have to come to school before?" she asked.

"I had lessons at home. So I could help my pa."

"Help your pa? Every day?"

More like every night, I thought. I just nodded. She kept looking down at me. With the sun straight behind her it was hard to see her face.

"Everybody is talking about you," she said. "They thought you were new in town. I told them you were just new to civilization."

"Thanks." I wasn't sure if that was nice or not.

"I said your pa was a bank robber, and you helped him carry the loot, and you couldn't come to school because you were always on the run from the law."

It hit me then that maybe she knew we were shiners. Maybe her grandpa had told her. Or maybe she was kidding me. I hadn't been around a lot of girls, but I had always heard to be careful around them.

"Ain't you going to ask if I'm serious?" she said.

I still couldn't see her face because of the sun, but her voice sounded like she was smiling.

"No," I said.

We were both quiet for a moment, Rebecca scratching her bare leg with her shoe. She seemed to be waiting for something, and I didn't know what to say.

"I hated those candies at your house," I said finally. "I about puked 'em up. I ate one and threw the other in a badger hole."

She laughed. "I don't like them either. Grandpa keeps 'em in a box from before the war. There's ants in the box," she said with a giggle. A teacher on the side yard called us all back inside.

As we headed for the door together, Rebecca turned to me and asked, "What did you have to help your pa with anyways?"

Before I could make up a story, two older kids stepped in front of us. One of them had hair and eyebrows the color of red clay. The other had hair cut so short he looked bald. Probably because of head lice. I could see over his shoulder that everybody else had gone inside the school.

43

"Your name Jennings?" the red-haired one asked me. He had a face as plain as a piece of lumber.

I nodded.

"My folks told me about your pa. Say he's not respectable. Makes moonshine. A criminal."

"That ain't true," I said back.

"You saying my pa's a liar? He's preacher at Beckwith Methodist, and if you call him a liar, I'll bash your face in."

I stood there thinking back if I had called his pa a liar, and then started wondering if bashing someone's face in was "respectable." But I had never been one for arguing and I didn't want to get beat up or get lice, so I put on my best confused face and asked, "What's moonshine anyways?"

Red Hair looked at me hard. "I don't rightly know."

Rebecca giggled, and Red Hair said, "Shut it, gravedigger."

She raised a fist and looked over the top of it at him. "Don't think I won't whup you."

The bald-headed kid snorted and said, "You've got a big mouth for a girl."

Rebecca turned to him and cocked her other fist up. "I got one for you too, ugly."

They stared hard at me, then turned and went inside.

I stood there with my leg tapping up a storm from nerves, trying to keep my breathing calm. I looked over at Rebecca, and her face was all red. She looked a little embarrassed, but mostly good and mad. I probably looked like I was about to have a heart attack.

"I hate that name 'gravedigger.' And stupid Shane thinks he runs the school," she said.

"I thought the teachers ran the school."

Rebecca rolled her eyes and tugged at my arm.

"Come on, we'll catch a whipping if we're late."

I ran in the door behind Rebecca, thinking how Miss Pounder could probably swing a switch like Babe Ruth and hoping I didn't have any more troubles with Shane or Bald-Head. It was pretty plain by then that there was more to school than the classes.

CHAPTER
6

BY THE THIRD DAY OF SCHOOL, I realized that my old suspicions about my home tutor, Miss Avery, having wasted my time with nonsense were correct. The other students were a lot more bookish. Arithmetic came easy to me, but the first reading examination came back to me so red it looked like it had been in a hatchet fight.

Rebecca's desk was right in front of mine, and I whispered to her, "Somebody drew red crosses all over my paper."

Out of the corner of her mouth she whispered back, "That was Miss Pounder."

Pounder had done this? I shot her a dirty look from my stump.

"Can she do that?" I whispered.

"For crying out loud, Cub. It's so you know you got them wrong."

I stuffed the paper in my front pocket.

"Well, I knew that when we *took* the test."

Even buck-toothed little Myrtle was out-reading me, and she

was only ten. And when I tried to pay attention, my thoughts would drift to the sheriff or wondering who else knew Pa shined. Time and time again Miss Pounder would catch my attention elsewhere and force me to stand up and rack my brain for some answer that had never been in there in the first place. She seemed to take a sick kind of pleasure in watching me embarrass myself.

That day we got our normal break from book time—recess, they called it—and were all shepherded outdoors, where I usually sat by myself in the shade of the schoolhouse. I was watching everyone else run around and laugh when the bald-headed guy, Jackson, called over to me.

"Hey, Cub! Come play Black Tuesday."

He hadn't bothered me since him and Shane said they were going to bash my face in, but I didn't trust him for a second. I shook my head no.

"Come on, don't be so yellow. We only got three, and you need at least four for Black Tuesday."

I studied him and his group as he itched at his scalp. There were indeed only three of them: Jackson, Frankie with the weird ears, and chubby Oliver who wore glasses. They were standing beside a long stick laid out in the grass. Next to the stick were three brown bags.

"Nah," I said.

Jackson threw his hands up in desperation and walked over.

When he was out of earshot of the other two, he whispered, "Dang it, Cub. I'm about to win Oliver's lunch off him. All you gotta do is run faster than him, and we'll be eating biscuits with molasses for lunch. We split it three ways, you, me, and Frankie."

For lunch I had only brought a boiled egg and a potato pancake the size of a half dollar. I snuck a quick peek at Oliver, who was digging in his ear with his pinky finger.

"What's the game?" I asked.

"Black Tuesday. It's a footrace. From that stick to the maple tree, loser gives up his lunch to the gold, silver, and bronze medalists."

I'd watched the kids race before and knew I was quicker than almost all of them.

"All right."

Jackson clapped his hands and whispered, "It's good molasses. His family's rich. Now go fetch your lunch and we'll start."

I ran into the schoolhouse to warm my legs up and was back in under twenty seconds. I put my bag down with theirs.

Oliver asked, "What's in your bag?"

I told the group, but didn't mention that the potato pancake was so little it wouldn't feed a mouse.

Jackson announced, "For Black Tuesday we got an egg and a potato pancake, biscuits and molasses, Frankie's fatback, and my corn bread."

"Plus my corn fritters," said Rebecca, walking up and thrusting her bag at Jackson.

I smiled at her, but she ignored me.

Jackson shook his head and didn't take the bag.

"That's too many then. Not enough food for the winners."

"Yeah, but I'm putting up nine fritters," she said.

Jackson rolled his eyes as Rebecca set her bag down with others.

"Fine, just line up."

I positioned myself between Jackson and Oliver, dead ahead of the maple tree. It wasn't but a hundred yards away, and I could feel my muscles twitching to get running.

Jackson edged me over and put his foot right behind the stick.

"On *Black Tuesday,* we go. Gotta touch the tree with your hand."

Everyone leaned out over the stick. I could feel my heart pumping hard already.

Jackson called out, "One, two, three, Black Tuesday!"

Head down, I shot out from behind the line as fast as I could.

I heard someone yell "Crash!" and then my legs went out from under me and I was flying. I couldn't even get one hand down to brace myself and skidded on my face and stomach, legs bent up backwards behind me. I nearly flipped all the way over.

As I stood and tried to figure out what had happened, I heard everyone howling with laughter. My shin throbbed, and for a second I thought I'd stumbled over the starting-line stick, but when I looked ahead and saw Jackson almost doubled over with laughter, I realized he'd tripped me.

I stood there like an idiot as Frankie reached the tree. Oliver strolled in for second place. Rebecca and Jackson had both stopped completely about fifty yards from the maple. Rebecca was looking back at me. Jackson was doubled over with his hands on his knees, about to bust a gut laughing.

"You see his legs go up?" Jackson cried. "He was bent in half! Looked like a scorpion's tail coming up!"

I didn't know what else to do, so I started running, not home like I wanted, but toward the tree.

Jackson laughed even harder at my efforts and jogged toward the tree. Rebecca paused a second, then started running again too. No matter how hard I ran, there was no way I could catch either of them.

Right as Jackson slapped the maple tree, I heard a yell. I looked over and saw Rebecca hopping on one foot and clutching at her hamstring.

She'd cramped up. I started to veer toward her to go see if she was all right, but didn't want to look like a sissy so I kept running. I still had about fifty yards to go, but she was just hopping in circles, and I was flying across the yard. In five seconds I'd be at the tree.

Five seconds later I wasn't at the tree. I was standing next to her asking if she was all right.

She stopped hopping and glared at me.

"Run, you knucklehead."

"But your leg," I stammered.

"Run, or I'm gonna kick you in the head with it."

She made no sense, but I ran and touched the maple bark.

Scowling at Jackson, I said, "That was a rotten trick."

"That's the game, idiot," he said. Oliver was already bringing the lunch bags so we could divvy up the prize. I looked over and saw Rebecca walking back toward the schoolhouse. She wasn't even going to finish the race. I could give her my share of her fritters back, but she'd probably just throw them in my face and threaten to neck punch me or something so maybe I wouldn't.

Jackson said, "Give me the fritters," snatching Rebecca's bag from Oliver.

I held out my hand, waiting, but suddenly Jackson heaved Rebecca's bag of fritters across the field at her. She was way out of range, so the bag hit the grass. I smiled as a bunch of pinecones rolled out.

Back in the schoolhouse after recess, I leaned over and said, "That was a good one you pulled in the race. You should've seen Jackson's face."

She turned around in her desk, not smiling.

"You need to wise up. I only helped you because I can't stand Jackson."

"I think you did it because you're a good person. I don't care what everybody says, I think you're all right."

She spun completely around, looking indignant.

50

"Who said . . ."

I grinned at her and her words trailed off.

"Ha. I got you," I said.

She rolled her eyes and gave me the tiniest smile before turning back around.

That week I watched Rebecca, trying to figure her out. I could not. In the span of three days she ate lunch with three different groups of people, slapped seven people across the back of the head, and cried because she only got nineteen out of twenty on the reading exam. And regarding me personally, I still couldn't tell if the pinecone trick was because she knew I was about to get hustled, or because she wanted to see us all eat pinecone.

On Friday afternoon, I walked home in a strong fall breeze, relieved to put the constant chatter of the schoolhouse behind me. The jumble of noises there made me feel like I was inside a hornet's nest. As I cut off Elm Street onto the dirt road home, the silence was interrupted by the *putt-putt-putt* of a motor. There weren't but four or five automobiles in Hidden Orchard, and save for the occasional lost traveler or door-to-door Bible salesman, outsiders seldom came through in a car.

I turned and saw the shiny grille of a Model A creeping up behind me. The glare off the windshield made it hard to see the driver's face, but I could make out the outline of a big cowboy hat. It was Sheriff Bardo. I stopped walking, praying Pa wasn't in the back of the car in handcuffs. The car pulled up next to me, and the sheriff's smiling face appeared in the window. He was alone.

"Ever been inside a car?" he asked.

"No, sir."

"You're in luck then. I'll take you for a ride."

I paused.

"No, thank you, sir."

The smile dropped off the sheriff's face, and he said, "I've never heard of a boy who didn't like cars. Especially one for catching bad guys. Get in."

He flung the passenger-side door open. It wasn't an offer, but an order. I walked around the front and climbed in.

I banged the door shut and looked around. A thick wooden steering wheel stuck out from the front and reached almost to the sheriff's belly. Gauges and levers and dials were everywhere, and the sheriff made a big show of adjusting and maneuvering them and stamping his foot, but we didn't move. The sheriff frowned and mashed a foot pedal down in a roar and wiggled some kind of driving stick with his hand. Something finally caught because the car shuddered and we went bucking down the dirt road. A month ago, being inside of a car would have been aces. Sitting next to the sheriff now, I felt caged.

We rambled down the road with only the loud chugging of the engine. Even with the two windows down, the sour metallic smell of oil filled the air.

"You doing good in school?" the sheriff yelled.

"Not really, sir," I yelled back.

"I guess you can't help your father anymore," he said, looking over at me.

I looked down and swallowed hard. If I thought fast, I could spin something believable.

"School lets out late October so students can help with the harvest. I can help him farm then."

He laughed. "'Farm.' Your pa tell you to lie like that?"

I didn't answer.

The sheriff was no fool. And he had us pegged. I sat there watching the cornstalks bounce by and wondering if he was really taking me home or we were just stopping to pick up Pa before we went to the jail.

The sheriff went on, "If you continue down the path you're on, I'll make it my business to get you straightened out. Get you away from that bad influence."

The automobile was crushing in on me, and I was feeling so trapped I wanted to throw myself out the window. We were just one turn away from the house.

The sheriff said, "You realize if he goes to jail, you don't go with him. You'd go into the orphanage."

The car lurched forward and I threw my hands up to stop myself. The sheriff had braked to a complete stop right at the drive to our house. I pressed on the door to get out, but it wouldn't open. The sheriff started laughing, but even when I threw my shoulder into the door, it wouldn't budge. I had no idea how to get out. He was laughing harder now, almost drowning out the rumble of the engine as he reached over me and released an opening latch with his hand.

I jumped out and took off running down the drive. I ran as fast as I could, straight past the house. And as I sprinted out behind the eastern field, a thought hit me that was so traitorous I thought it might break me mid-stride—it wasn't just the sheriff I wanted to get away from. It was shining and Pa too.

CHAPTER 7

THE WIND WAS SHARPER near the woods, and the cold air filled my lungs like creek water as I gasped for breath. I dropped down next to Ma's grave and tried to stop my jaw from rattling. With my knees to my chest, I sat motionless and wordless for the better part of an hour, visions of the sheriff's Model A, Pa's candles lit inside the tree, and my classmates' stares all whirling through my head.

When I had calmed a bit, I rolled over onto my side and faced the gravestone. At the base were some morning glories tied up with red string Pa must have left recently.

"I'm not going anywhere. I don't care what orphanages or jails they try to put us in."

I picked up the flowers and rolled the stems back and forth in my fingers. "Without you around, me and Pa have got to look out for each other. I mind him and do what he says because he's all I've got."

Shaking my head, I added, "But this is about more than just

shining now. It's about splitting us up. And he's not doing anything to help."

The orphanage, jail—it all meant the same thing. And for the first time, I could see it clearly. We were shining our way right out of a family.

When I got back to the house, Pa asked where I'd been. And for the first time I could recollect, I considered fibbing to him. It had been a shameful day at school and in that police car, and for once I didn't want to confide in Pa. I even started to think up a story about fishing by the old bridge, but other words poured out of me. I came clean about Sheriff Bardo, the orphanage, even about how I hadn't done the best job denying we were shiners.

Pa just rocked back and forth in his rickety wooden chair, looking past me with his jaw clenched firm. As the sun went down past the lowest corner of the kitchen window, I lit the lamp and we shared a small piece of salted pork and a boiled potato. The meal sat heavy in my stomach.

"Don't worry. I'm going to handle this," Pa said.

"How?"

If he had a plan, now was the time to tell me.

"Hard work. It'll get you through anything."

"So the plan is to shine more?" I asked.

That was not the plan I had in mind. In fact it was about the exact opposite.

I said, "What if we stopped for a while. 'Til springtime?"

"Stop? Nobody's stopped us from shining for twelve years now, I'm proud to say. Just because things get tough, it doesn't mean you tuck your tail and run," he said with a shake of his finger.

As we finished eating, he said, "I'd thought maybe you'd want to work tonight since you ain't got school tomorrow, but we can stay in if you're still too shook up. The mash can hold for a day or two."

I stared down at my cracked wooden plate. I could feel Pa waiting for me to say something.

"We should go shine," I said.

"No, not tonight," he said. "Not unless you want to, I mean."

"I want to," I said quietly.

Pa pushed his chair back and slapped his hands together. His clap popped like a .22 inside our little cabin, and I nearly jumped out of my seat.

"That's it, boy! Can't nobody spook a Jennings!"

I was spooked, though. I was spooked good because it looked like one of us was dead set on being as reckless as possible. And the other was too gutless to tell him.

Around midnight, we walked the worn path through the woods, following the yellow glow of an old railroad lantern Pa held up in front of us. In the clearing, I crumbled deadwood from a pine log under the giant kettle, and it caught easily with the first match.

We were behind our normal schedule, and as I watched Pa struggle to drag over an eighty-pound sack of cornmeal, I realized just how hard the past weeks had been for him. He had double work now since I had to sleep most nights on account of school. With the fire running hot and the steam cap fitted down tightly on the boiler, we sat down on the pine needles. We leaned against the old log, legs stretched out toward the fire just like we had done a million times before. Even so, I didn't feel normal. I felt almost like an outsider there now, which was exactly how I felt at school too.

"Pa, you ever think about living somewhere else?" I asked.

He opened one eye and asked, "You mean like leaving here?"

"I don't know."

"Mmm, well, I did live somewhere else once. Me and your ma had a beautiful place. Big old farm."

"Where?" I asked.

We were both talking into the fire, leaning back against the log.

"Not far from here. Out towards Yunsen's."

"How come you never took me to see it?" I asked.

"It's a little sad for me."

Pa leaned his head up off the log and tossed a little rock into the flames. He was remembering hard, I could tell. I let him take his time with it.

"It was so nice there," he said finally. "The dirt was perfect. Your mother would bring in tomatoes from the garden as big as your head. And there was a pond too, with bass in it. They weren't too big, but big enough."

He chuckled, his words now spilling out. "And corn like you wouldn't believe. Bushels to sell, corn bread almost every night, a big pumpkin patch."

Most of the kids at school came from farming families. They weren't rich, but they were fed. And they didn't have to worry about going to jail.

"What happened?" I asked.

"A little cough happened. Your mother took sick with consumption. We tried all the treatments. Went to Memphis, went to Nashville. Took the train to Atlanta. Sold that farm so we'd have money so she could be cured."

"She wasn't cured though," I said.

"No, she wasn't. It would come and it would go, and then it never left. But something happened while she was sick."

"What?"

"She got pregnant with you."

I turned toward Pa, and I could see the shadows moving on his face as he smiled.

"She was scared you were going to be sick too, but you came out strong. Doctor himself said you were a miracle."

He settled back against the log. I was quiet, my thoughts on what to say rising and drifting away like the embers off the fire. It was hard to imagine Pa living anywhere but our little cabin, or really right there at the clearing. He'd been in a heck of a hard spot and done what he'd seen best. That was a long time ago, though. We sat for over an hour, Pa dozing and me thinking.

When he finally stirred and sat up, I asked, "Pa, what do you think Ma would say about shining?"

Pa rubbed a hand over his face and sighed. "I reckon she'd be happy I kept you from starving. Kept you here in Hidden Orchard."

"I don't think she'd like it."

Pa gave me a look and started to say something, but then all of a sudden his wrinkled face looked too tired to even argue.

The moon was sitting up above the far pines, so I knew it was about 3:30 in the morning. I could catch an hour of sleep here before we walked back home.

Pa moved the water bucket out from in front of the fire, and I pulled off the giant red flannel shirt we shared and pushed all the fabric down into one of the sleeves. With that shirt pillow under my head, I got comfortable there on the ground. Pa walked over and looked down on me.

"You're pretty creative with that shirt there. I mostly just use it for body-wearing," Pa said.

I smiled and said, "One time I made it into a pillow and a blanket. Can't remember how I did it though."

"This year I'll get you one of your own. A brand-new flannel from Grayson's downtown."

He had been saying that on cold nights for years.

"It's okay, Pa. I don't mind sharing."

"I know you don't," he said quietly and walked back around the fire.

I closed my eyes and tried to figure if everybody who broke the law could put such good reasoning behind why they did it. And if the reasoning was good, were they really criminals? Or were they just fooling themselves?

Pa nudged me awake before the roosters crowed, and we didn't say a word on the walk home. The lantern burned itself out, but the sky was still bright and fuzzied up with stars. Pa was going slow so I walked on past thinking how if he had gotten into shining because of me in the first place, then maybe I'd have to be the one to get him out of it too.

CHAPTER
8

MOST EVERY GUY BUT ME PLAYED in the lunchtime kickball game. They would play with a lopsided ragball in the dirt scrub behind the schoolhouse, while I sat by myself under an ash tree. Besides that Black Tuesday game, where I got my legs kicked out from under me, I hadn't made much of an effort to join any of the games. These recesses and lunches were getting harder, though, because it didn't feel so good always being alone. I'd even asked Pa what to do in those recess times, and he just said, "Run around, chase girls, play ball. Normal stuff."

I figured the kickball game was my best bet. I'd even walked up to join once, but changed my mind at the last minute and instead wandered between third base and shortstop like a moron before veering off through the dandelions in left field with everyone staring at me. After seeing bowlegged Bobby Ray ground it back to the pitcher like he did every at bat, I decided today was going to be different.

I finished my cheese sandwich and walked over to Russ, the captain of the kicking team. He was off the first-base side getting ready to bat and watching the bottom of the first inning.

"Russ, you think I could get in the game?"

He turned halfway toward me, trying to keep one eye on the field.

"You know how to play?"

"Sure. I am a champion player," I said, not knowing a thing.

"All right, then. Pinch-hit for Bobby Ray next time up."

I was walking behind the catcher to wait my turn when I heard yelling.

"No, no, no! He's not playing. He'll try to steal the ball or something."

Shane, the redheaded preacher's son, was sprinting in from right field.

He ran up on me and Russ, pointing and shaking his head. "Don't let him play. His pa's a drunk and a criminal, and he's no better."

"He is not!" I said.

Shane got in my face, and I was looking straight up into his chin whiskers. The game stopped and everyone in the yard ran up to circle around us.

"He's not playing," Shane said to Russ, then turned to me and said, "We don't want your kind here. My pa told me what kind of trash you Jennings are."

"Yeah, well, I heard your pa uses the collection-plate money to buy hog feed for your ma."

To be honest, I had never heard anything about anyone, but I was starting to understand how this game was played.

Shane did not flinch at my dig. In fact, he smiled bigger, like he was happy I'd fought back.

He leaned in and said, "Well, my pa says the best thing about your family is that most of it's dead."

He could have said anything he pleased about me, and I likely would've ended up slinking out of there with my tail between my legs. But he wasn't talking about just me. Those words burned like fire, and I decided to kill him right there and then, preacher's son and all.

I rocked back on my right leg, loaded up my right hand, and before I even knew what was happening, I had swung on him. I pivoted good in the dirt and just pistoned my right hand straight down the pipe and into his breadbasket. I put my heart and soul into that punch, and it hit him square in the gut, knocking him back maybe a quarter of an inch.

Next thing I knew, I was on the ground getting walloped on and everybody was yelling and there was dust all in my eyes and I could taste blood hot in my mouth. Shane was sitting on top of my chest with my arms pinned under his knees, and I couldn't wriggle free. He was hollering something or other and just punching and punching on my face. When I opened my eyes and could see through all the dust and the punches, he looked like he'd gone out of his head. He was slobbering and crying and yelling as he rained down punches on me. Then Miss Pounder had me by the ear and was dragging me out of the circle.

I don't recollect the next part too good on account of being in a daze, but I heard the door slam behind her, and before long she had a hickory switch in her hand and was wailing on my backside and the backs of my legs. I just slumped over her desk and let her finish off what Shane had started. That was the first switching of my entire life. Shane wasn't going to get one, supposedly because I'd hit first. I wondered if it was more because of who his father was.

Miss Pounder gave me a minute to get myself together before calling the class in, and I tried to wiggle around on my stump seat to find a way to sit there that didn't feel like my pants were on fire.

I looked up, and she was staring at me from behind that big desk of hers, shaking her head.

She said, "I can't imagine how confusing all this is for you, having lived hidden away your whole life."

I squirmed around some more and nodded.

"It's just so many things I didn't know, and I can't learn it all fast enough."

Miss Pounder went out to clang the bell, but my class was already pouring in, all babbling about the fight. And for once, folks were actually making an effort to sit near me, if only to have a better view of my lumps. Shane walked in scowling, but we didn't make eye contact and he sat on the far side of the room.

Russ gave me a half smile and said, "Good game, huh?"

"I told you I was a champion player. I got lots of hits."

He chuckled, and I laughed a little too, just so I wouldn't cry.

"'Lots of hits,' he says. Well, you did, but maybe next time go for hits on the field instead of hits on your face."

Russ had said "next time," which was a speck of hope on a hopeless day, but then Shane's buddy Jackson came up and ruined it.

"You're even uglier than before," he said, and pressed his dirty finger into a bump on my forehead.

I pushed his hand away and tried to think of a comeback, but my brain was rattled from the brawl and I said nothing.

Rebecca, however, leaned back from her desk and said, "Those little scrapes aren't nothing. Cub popped him in the gut. Shane only got face shots in. The gut is where the real damage is done."

There was a murmur in the class as people considered this.

Rebecca added, "Matter fact, Cub won that scrap."

The murmurs turned to scoffs and laughter, and I hung my head.

Shane said, "That's dumber than dumb. Even for you, gravedigger."

Jackson and Shane were well aware that calling Rebecca "gravedigger" was her one weak spot. I guess she was like me in that family insults cut deep.

This time though, she just smiled and said, "How do you think I know so much about gut shots? When a dead body comes in from a beating, nine times out of ten it's from a hit to the innards. That's where all the kidneys and vitals are. Maybe you won't feel the pain at first, but then one day, boom! You're dead."

Someone gasped, and the class's attention swung to Shane, who was on the other side of the room sulking. Rebecca's opinion on such matters was highly respected, and though I knew I had definitely lost the fight, I was glad the attention was off me until Miss Pounder finally came in and I could make it through the rest of the day.

I arrived home not really walking straight because of the switching, and then Pa of course asked why my face was bumped up. I told him a rough version of what had happened—that I had gotten into a ruckus playing ball. There was no need to trouble him with details. He laughed and put his hand on my head and mussed up my hair and just walked out back to the still. I stood there gritting my teeth and waited for the pain to pass from him shaking my throbbing head.

The rest of the week at school, folks still didn't say much to me. Miss Pounder was strict as ever. The only thing Shane said to me was that his preacher father was going to make sure I went to hell. The excitement over the fight died down, but when the topic did come up, Rebecca was quick to remind people of my big punch. She was the only person I felt halfway natural around, and she could talk like nobody's business, which somehow put me at ease. Even so, sometimes I wondered if she actually liked being around me or just pitied me like I was some stray dog. Either way, I was glad to have the company.

We took to walking home together down Elm until our paths split, then we'd stand there under the big yellow poplar, talking. From time to time the chugging of a car would sound in the distance, and I'd edge farther off the road, praying the sheriff wouldn't come while I was with her.

I listened for that mechanical rumble constantly, straining my ears to make sure it was nowhere near. That Wednesday while helping Pa rake out the henhouse, I heard it. We both froze at the sound, Pa cocking his head up like a startled whitetail. The noise was close, practically on top of us, then stopped.

"Get inside," Pa whispered.

As he crept around the corner toward the front of the house, I ran in the back door, straight to the front window to see who had come.

It wasn't the sheriff's Model A. It was a long, sleek vehicle, dark and expensive-looking. Its glossed-up fender was sitting nearly on top of the front porch. A hefty man with slicked-back hair stood watching Pa stumble around the side of our house, brushing chicken feathers off his overalls. The stranger wore a formal suit and was leaning coolly against his vehicle. He did not look like police.

I could not make out a word between them, the stranger apparently doing all the talking while Pa shuffled back and forth in front of him in the dirt. Slowly I saw Pa's face relax a bit and the trace of a smile appeared as he turned and headed for the front door. I darted away from the window before he could catch me spying. I stood as calmly as my twitching muscles would let me.

"Are we in trouble, Pa?"

Pa chuckled and shook his head.

"No, no. Fella with an interesting proposition."

He crossed into the kitchen and ladled some water into a glass jar.

"What's he want?" I asked.

"Ah, just some business. Clears a lot of things up."

"What things, Pa?" I nearly yelled. His calmness was giving me a fit.

He took a sip of the water and looked down at me. "Want to come out?"

The stranger had already seated himself in one of our rockers on the porch when we went out. Pa handed the water to the man and then sat next to him in the other chair. The man took a sip and set the glass jar on the very edge of the porch railing. I stood between the door and Pa.

"How you doing, kid?" the stranger asked as he rocked slowly back and forth. His gut slumped down almost between his knees. It was hard not to look at it.

"You look like a man who has a sweet tooth, am I right?" he asked, closing one eye and pointing a finger at me.

I nodded and smiled. He smiled back, his ruddy cheeks squeezing up into his eyes.

He shook his finger at me and said, "I knew it, I knew it. I can always spot a fellow candy man."

He pulled a plastic bag of candies out of his coat pocket and offered them to me. They were store-bought caramel creams, wrappers and everything.

"Thank you, sir," I said, taking one for me and one for Pa.

The man smiled even bigger. He had a hair tonic on his head that looked greasier than warm lard.

"Soon enough your pop here is going to be able to get you all the candies you want," he said.

Pa laughed and waved a dirty hand in the air. "Hold on there, mister. Let's not get too ahead of ourselves before we talk money."

The man acted like Pa hadn't even spoke and kept looking at me.

"He'll get you some Slo Pokes. Some Almond Roca. Big bag of Violet Mints."

I turned and looked at Pa, hoping he would say something. Rocking back on my heels, I wished I hadn't come out.

"This here is Mr. Salvatore. He's from up North," Pa said finally.

"I was just offering your pop here an opportunity to make some money. Big stacks of it."

"Doing what?" I asked.

"Making liquor," Mr. Salvatore said.

"We don't do that," I said as fast as I could.

Mr. Salvatore leaned over and slapped Pa's leg like they were old friends.

"You taught him well!" he said.

I thought I saw Pa kind of flinch at the touch. His face was still calm, but his eyes looked uneasy. Or maybe it was just me feeling that way. This Salvatore guy certainly looked comfortable, though, and sure wasn't scared to speak his mind.

"Your pop here said the same thing at first," Mr. Salvatore said. "But a little birdie told me you cooked up something special here. Your own blend. A secret flavor."

"A family recipe," Pa said.

"What flavor?" Mr. Salvatore asked.

"I'm afraid that information is for customers."

Mr. Salvatore eyed him hard, but didn't press.

"Can you do fifty gallons?"

Pa brushed his hair back over his ears and smiled.

"We've already got over eight hundred."

Salvatore stopped rocking and looked at him with renewed interest. He leaned toward him with his forearms resting on his knees. A clunky gold watch slid out from under his cuff and rested against his meaty hand.

"You'd be working for me directly. The law won't bother you. You work hard and provide what I need, you'll be a lot better off

67

than you are now." He flicked his wrist and waved his hand at our little cabin.

Pa shook his head and said, "I don't think you know the law around here. They don't care much for shining. Told us that a couple times now."

Mr. Salvatore laughed. "Oh, I know 'em, all right. Sheriff Bardo. And I know he told you to stop shining. I've convinced him otherwise. He's not going to make trouble. I get the liquor I need and things go on just like they always have."

I wondered if this man was telling the truth. Would the sheriff leave us alone? If anybody knew how to get around police, I reckoned it would be this fella.

Mr. Salvatore went on, "So it's your lucky day. You get to be a part of my operation. And since you're working for me directly, I make sure the sheriff leaves you alone."

I looked at Pa, who was staring at the floorboards and pressing his lips together. He looked like he was fighting to keep a smile off his face, which seemed crazy because I was fighting to keep from running out of there. No one spoke for a long time, the only sound the dry creaking of Salvatore's rocker.

Pa said finally, "We appreciate the offer, sir. It's mighty generous of you. I will of course need some time to think it through."

Mr. Salvatore stared hard at him, then turned to me and smiled.

"Tell your pop here not to be foolish."

I looked back at him and thought how all day at school, every day and every night, how I had been just praying for a way to keep the sheriff away. And the solution had driven right up our drive and was now sitting on our front porch. The sheriff would disappear, and we'd keep on shining like nothing had ever happened, and it was all just such a perfect way to keep from having to change that it made me want to throw up.

"He's not foolish," I said to Mr. Salvatore.

I looked into his eyes and saw a man capable of great violence. He did not reply, but rose and straightened his suit.

"You think about what I said. I've got some other people to see. I'll be back Wednesday," he said.

His black dress shoes tapped on the porch boards as he walked away. He slid behind the wheel of that big black automobile, backed away from the porch, and sped off down the drive.

"I hate when people come here," I said. "Hate it more than anything."

Pa jumped up out of his rocker, laughing, and clapped his hands together.

"Ooh boy, you see that poker face I put on? 'I'll have to think about it,' I says to him."

"Are you going to think about it?" I asked.

"Heck, no. Ain't nothing to think about. This gets Sheriff Bardo off our backs! And we'll have big money coming in. No more piddling half-pint sales, no more struggling to scrape by and having to share clothes. Our troubles are over!"

"I don't mind sharing, Pa," I said, but he was off in his own world.

He was skipping back and forth on the porch and I thought he was liable to dance a jig. I stood there silent, looking at the corn, and beyond it the dust cloud trailing Mr. Salvatore's car. I thought of him being our new boss for the rest of our lives and hoped he crashed that fancy car of his a couple hundred times before he came back on Wednesday.

CHAPTER 9

EVEN THOUGH IT WAS STILL DAYLIGHT, I went into my room and lay down on my scratchy red blanket and stared up at the crooked ceiling beams. This Mr. Salvatore said he could keep the sheriff away. So why did it seem so bad? Why had my gut seized up like that when Mr. Salvatore patted Pa's leg?

That evening Pa and I ate our supper with barely a word between us.

I finally asked, "Is that man a criminal?"

He sighed and said, "I reckon he is. But he's nothing I can't handle."

To Pa, there was nothing he couldn't handle. You'd tell him he had to wrestle a grizzly and he'd say, "Only one?" But now I was starting to wonder if he really believed all his blustering or if he just acted so hard so I wouldn't worry.

"He looks like one of the gangsters from the papers."

Pa laughed. "I'm sure he'd be just pleased as pie to hear somebody say that."

"What if we didn't do it, Pa?" I said suddenly. "What if we told him no?"

Pa stared at me wide-eyed, chicken thigh still held up to his mouth.

"You hit your head or something?" he asked, then started talking fast. "So I tell him no, and then what? Then the sheriff puts me in jail? Puts you in some orphanage? What kind of plan is that?"

"It's not a plan, Pa. It's just I don't particularly like having to listen to Mr. Salvatore or the sheriff."

"I don't particularly like doing a lot of things, but I reckon I'd like being in jail a lot less. Don't you understand what would happen to me? To us?"

"I do," I said softly.

"Or you don't care?" he asked, then went back to his chicken thigh.

I did care. But I also cared that there was a difference between shining to get by and working for some crook from up North. I knew it inside me. As I looked at the chicken bones on my plate, I wondered about Mr. Salvatore's offer. What if it had been like the sheriff's offer to ride in the car—not something that could be turned down?

Pa got up and picked the bones off our plates and tossed them out the back door. He sat back down and patted my head. "Change is hard. But this is a good thing. And I'll be the one dealing with him, you don't have to worry."

So that was his angle. He figured no matter how bad it was, as long as it was on his shoulders and not mine, it was all right. He still thought he had to do everything for us.

I forced a smile at him.

"I'm glad you understand. Now tell me, you liking school?"

The jump from thinking about gangsters and police to school

71

and Miss Pounder threw me for a second, and I didn't rightly know what to say.

"Mmm, sometimes we learn good stuff, like about buffalo and the old days."

Pa asked, "You getting along with the kids there?" He leaned back and gave me a big smile and added, "Besides that one fella you pounded on?"

"It ain't exactly easy," I said, then paused for a second. "I mean it wasn't at first. Now I've got lots of pals."

"I am glad to hear that. I was a touch worried I'd waited too long for your schooling and whatnot. Afraid you'd be like that coyote, acting all wild and ignorant."

It's not like that at all, I thought. People would probably want to spend time with the coyote.

"No, Pa. I've got lots of friends. Ten. A whole gang of 'em," I lied.

He beamed at me and asked, "And are you doing okay with your learning?"

"Fair. Except for reading. Mr. Yunsen's granddaughter said she could help me if I wanted."

After I'd flunked my fourth reading test in a row, she'd offered to practice with me.

"Ah, Rebecca."

In a high-pitched voice he squeaked, "'Hi, Cub. I'm Re-bec-ca,'" his voice cracking right in the middle of the impression.

"You'd make a terrible girl, Pa," I said with a laugh.

I hesitated for a moment and then continued. "She said I could go to her house day after next so she could help me with reading."

"I think that's a fine idea. And I'll tell you what. This morning I saw that the blackberries out by the clearing were still good for picking. I'll bring you some and you can take 'em over there as a courtesy."

• • •

That next morning in arithmetic, Jackson got caught talking while Miss Pounder was writing problems on the board and she lit into him like I couldn't believe. Rebecca had warned me that Miss Pounder was known to fly off the handle when folks tried to talk while she had her back turned. I thought she had exaggerated quite a bit, but that morning I saw the fury myself, as Miss Pounder stopped just short of body-slamming Jackson.

For once I was not the spectacle and actually enjoying the show, but Pounder finished with Jackson and set her sights on me. She barked out my name and rapped on the blackboard with her knuckles. She and the whole class watched me squint up at the board and try to figure on the problem.

$$\begin{array}{r} 18 \\ \times\ 6 \\ \hline \end{array}$$

Standing by my stump seat, I thought about the night last March when me and Pa filled 18 jugs before dawn. That was Monday. Two more nights of the same work and by sunup Thursday we had put 54 jugs in the tree. So three nights was 54. Double that to six nights and it's 108.

"A hundred and eight jugs," I said.

"What?" Miss Pounder asked.

"A hundred and eight, I mean."

"When I call on you, you're supposed to work it out on the board, but . . ."

She faltered, twisting her head back to the figures, then back to me, then to the board again.

"But let's just show the class how you arrived at that," she said, turning her back to the room and hacking away at the board. She finally stepped to the side to display a 108 in a small cloud of chalk dust. I took that as the sign that I could sit back down. The rest of the class stared at me as curious as ever.

Little Myrtle behind me whispered, "You knew that one before Miss Pounder did."

I turned to nod to her, flinching slightly at the sight of her giant choppers.

"Thanks, Myrtle," I whispered back.

"That's not a good thing, ya dunce."

School passed slowly that day, but I guarded the brown bag of blackberries close, not having but four myself at lunch. After classes Rebecca and I walked out of the schoolhouse together into a cool autumn day. As we cut into her yard full of rusted scrap metal, I thought that even her crumbling old house had a nice look to it, and I began to grin like a buffoon. As I spent more time away from home and Pa, I would occasionally stumble upon these strange feelings of freedom. A moment of joy would hit me out of nowhere, and I was eager for more of it.

"I'll show you something neat," Rebecca said as we neared the side of the house.

She tugged on the elbow of my shirtsleeve and led me around to the back. Where the front yard was all weeds and rust, the back was bare dirt, save for one of the most beautiful things I'd ever seen in my life. It sat there grand-looking with its nose angled back toward the house. I approached it cautiously and respectfully while Rebecca opened a back door and called inside.

"Grandpa, I'm home. I'm going to show Cub the Buick."

The vehicle was spotless, long and slick, midnight black with a touch of gold trim racing around the body.

"It's a '27 Buick," Rebecca said.

"It's double size."

"Has to be. For the caskets."

I had heard of these special cars but never seen one before, not even in a postcard picture. I inched forward and peeked in between the white lace curtains hanging inside the back windows. Sure enough, there was a chestnut casket in the back.

"Why is it at your house?" I asked.

"Grandpa works here. He's got a whole funeral parlor set up downstairs."

"With dead bodies?"

Rebecca nodded.

"And that doesn't scare you?"

She shrugged her shoulders and said, "It's a part of life, Grandpa says."

I frowned. I reckoned it was easy to think like that until someone close to you died.

She went on. "People spend so much time worrying about death, but it's all just a big circle. He says to look at it as a reminder to enjoy life."

I turned and asked, "Do you actually know anybody that's died?"

She dropped her head and started smoothing out her dress. "Let's go in. I should help you with the lesson."

We sat at the same big table where we'd first talked to Mr. Yunsen, only now I was in my pa's chair and Rebecca in her grandpa's. Rebecca was real quiet and had that sad-angry look on her face like when somebody called her "gravedigger." Before long, though, we had that bag of blackberries between us and were laughing and reading a story about a grandma and her pet wolf. I read out loud and Rebecca helped me sound out the longer words. Halfway through the story, our fingers, mouths, and the corners of the book's pages were stained purple. Miss Pounder was going to pitch a fit, but at that moment I didn't care.

"You've got such a big house," I said, looking up at the ceiling. Two of my houses could have fit in that one room.

"It's fun to play in. Except downstairs," she said and giggled.

"Me and my pa have just got a little place. The woods are big, but the house is small. Him and my ma used to live around here somewhere."

"I've been by there," she said, fluttering the book's pages.

"You have?" I couldn't believe she'd been there and I never had even once.

She frowned at me. "Sure. Grandpa showed me."

"What's it like?"

"You know, it's just a normal place. Nice."

"Normal," I said, trying to picture it.

We finished up reading and I realized I hadn't seen a single other person there at Rebecca's.

"Is your ma home?" I asked. I looked around the giant room, like I might spot her sitting silently in a corner.

"No."

"Your pa?"

"They don't live here. They're in Chicago so my pa could work. My uncle got him a job at a cigar factory. And my ma works too, washing clothes." She quickly added, "They're coming to visit soon."

I was a little sorry I'd opened my big mouth. Having your parents live far away was almost as bad as getting sent off to the orphanage. I only said, "That will be nice," and waited to see if she would go on. She did.

"You asked if I knew anybody that died and I do," she began, then sucked in a breath so sharply it sounded like she was choking. "I knew my little brother, Arthur. He was just a baby."

Her hands were trembling now and she was rustling the book's pages. I thought she might burst into tears and run out of the room.

"He got sick. So sick he got blinded and there was no money and he was always cold and he just couldn't get better. That's why my folks went to Chicago. My ma said it was to make sure nothing like that ever happened to me."

The tears were shining on her cheeks and my chest ached rotten.

She said, "I told 'em about a hundred times I didn't want them to go, but they wouldn't listen. With what happened to my baby brother . . ."

"My ma died too, a long time ago," I said quietly. "But I still miss her."

Rebecca leaned her head down so I wouldn't see her cry, but it was about as obvious as anything, especially when a fat tear plopped right down on the book. She kind of laughed through a big sniffle.

I smiled at her and said, "We ruined Miss Pounder's book." She laughed a little more and wiped her eyes.

We finished the blackberries, and I looked out the window and saw the shadows had gotten long. I said goodbye and walked out into the afternoon. Halfway down the Yunsens' gravel drive I realized that I now had a real friend at school.

Maybe it was a silly thing, but I couldn't help but smile. Not even the revelation that I had never actually had a friend before could break my spirit, and I cut toward town with my head high. I felt alive and strong and thought about how with the sheriff and Mr. Salvatore out of the way, I could make a real go at this new life.

I felt like I wasn't running scared anymore, and I was not afraid or even that surprised when I saw Mr. Salvatore's automobile parked in front of Grady's Soda Fountain. The first touch of fear did not come until I was standing beside his table, watching him spoon vanilla and caramel parfait into his mouth.

CHAPTER

10

Mr. Salvatore noticed me at his elbow and slowly unhunched himself from over his ice cream dish. Even seated he was taller than I was and seemed to be growing by the second.

"Get lost, kid. I got nothing on me."

"Excuse me, sir."

"I said I don't have any money. I gave my last two nickels to this swindler here," he said, aiming his words at old Mr. Grady behind the counter. Mr. Grady pretended not to hear, but his wrinkled face flushed pink and I felt even worse for him. He smoothed out his white apron and edged away to the far side of the counter to wash coffee mugs. There was no one else in the room, and the electric lights seemed too bright in there, everything shiny and reflecting off the mint-green countertops.

"Mr. Salvatore, this is about the other thing," I said, the words coming out of me before I had time to second-guess them.

He started at his name and looked me in the eyes for the first time. I spoke before he could.

"My father sends a message. Earl Jennings."

He glanced around the room to see if anyone was listening, then leaned over.

"I was heading there now," he said.

I whispered, "It's okay, sir. He says no, thank you."

I braced myself for bellowing and maybe even for him to strike me, but he just scraped caramel down the side of the dish and into the white blob of melted ice cream.

He swallowed it and wet his lips.

"Thought you said your pop wasn't foolish," he said.

I hadn't thought he was foolish before. Seeing how keen he was on working for this man, however, I didn't know what to think. And for once, I was doing something about it.

I shrugged and said again, "No, thank you."

"He is going to have a change of heart, kid," Mr. Salvatore said.

"Excuse me." I nodded to him and walked out before he could say another word.

The road no longer seemed a safe place to walk, so I took the long way home behind several neighboring farms. I'd had no intention of seeking out Mr. Salvatore and telling him no, but I'd somehow found the guts to do it. I'd gotten the nerve to finally make things happen myself, and yet I felt a hundred times worse than before. Why hadn't Salvatore just said okay? What if I'd made things worse?

Of course, I hadn't even considered what I'd say to Pa. I needed time to think, but my legs were filled with a nervous energy and the three and a half miles were finished too fast.

I got home and found Pa sitting on the front porch rocking just as furiously as he could. I had always thought rocking chairs were for relaxing, but Pa would jump on that thing and ride it like he was breaking a horse.

"Hey. I'm still waiting on Salvatore. I'm gonna negotiate him like you wouldn't believe."

Pa had on a pair of trousers he normally reserved for the Easter service and some fancy wing tips I'd never seen before.

"Where'd you get those shoes?"

He popped up with a grin and turned his feet side to side.

"Traded Old Man Weatherbee. I rubbed the scuffs out with a piece of coal. My negotiating shoes."

It was time to tell him what I'd told Salvatore. If not, Pa was liable to spend the whole night in the rocker waiting for him. Or until Mr. Salvatore came tearing up the drive and ran us both over.

"I don't think Mr. Salvatore is coming, Pa. I saw him in town. Leaving town, in fact."

He looked up from his new shoes with a hurt in his eyes that almost made me choke on my words.

"How do you know he was leaving?"

"I talked to him. He said the deal was off."

Pa dropped right back down into his chair like he'd been gunshot. He closed his eyes and put his fist to his forehead.

I said, "Maybe it ain't so bad. We don't need him, Pa. We'll be all right."

He shook his head, his carefully combed hair now falling all around his face.

"No, no, no. I'm so sorry, boy."

Don't say that, I thought. I feel bad enough.

He pounded his fist into his palm, still shaking his head back and forth.

"Me and my negotiating. I should have told him yes when I had the chance. I let you down."

"No, Pa. Not at all."

He got up and went into his room. I sat in the rocker and heard a pair of thumps that sounded like negotiating shoes being flung against the wall. Off in the distance, I saw an automobile speed past our drive and I wondered if I'd ever feel safe again.

When it got dark, I begged Pa to let me help him at the clearing, even though it was a school night. He was so distraught that he gave in without much fight. I felt a duty to him for not having been real honest and thought maybe my company would lift his spirits, but he just sulked down the trail as it got dark. He had changed out of his fancy clothes and looked normal again, but somehow twenty years older.

After getting the fire going, I poured Pa a generous drink and took it over to him. He stared down into the glass, then walked over and poured the shine right back into the barrel.

"Can't waste it on me. Going to have to find another big buyer now."

That night I did a week's worth of bottling, cleaning, and water hauling, but Pa didn't even seem to notice me rushing back and forth trying to help him. We finally stopped at what I guessed to be around three in the morning. Pa slumped down against the log and stared into the fire. I joined him.

"Salvatore had said he was going to come back," Pa said, not looking at me. "You heard him, right?"

"I don't remember exactly."

The dishonesty was just flowing out of me now.

"Why would he say that if he hadn't meant it? What kind of man tells a lie like that?"

I swallowed hard and thought, Don't talk about lies. Please.

We were silent for a while, my mind replaying my encounter with Mr. Salvatore in the ice cream parlor. He hadn't gotten mad. He'd stayed calm and cold like he always was. What had he said?

That Pa would have a "change of heart." He'd said it so certain, like he knew something we didn't. Maybe something related to the police.

My breath hitched and I put a hand to my forehead.

"Pa, do you think the sheriff is going to come back now?"

Pa rubbed a sooty hand over his face and sighed. "Probably."

I had not anticipated that. Had not even thought about Sheriff Bardo for a second.

To cover for myself, I quickly added, "I think it'll be okay. We'll figure a way out of this."

It was getting hard *not* to lie now.

My cheeks were getting warm, and I twisted away from the flames. Pa sat there like a stone.

Desperate to talk about something else, I said, "Can we take a trip tomorrow?"

"Where do you want to go?"

"To see that old house you and Ma used to live at."

He turned to me and frowned. "What for?"

"Just to see it, I don't know."

Pa faltered for a second, then said, "Fine, I don't care."

He rose to add more wood to the fire and asked me, "You want to take the lantern back? I can walk later without it."

"I'll just sleep here," I said, patting the worn spot in front of the log.

"I'll try and finish up early, then you can sleep some in your bed too before school."

Pa unbuttoned our red flannel and handed it to me, leaving himself in just a yellowed work shirt.

"No, Pa. It's cold out," I said.

He shook his head.

"That new one I was going to get you from Grayson's is going to have to wait a while. Use mine. I'm warm enough."

"Thanks. Night."

"Night."

I lay down against the log with that big red flannel shirt stretched out over me and the fire warming my face. In spite of everything, I actually still felt a speck of pride about having taken charge with Salvatore. I watched Pa as he worked and thought that maybe, just maybe, we would be all right after all. I was tired and soon dreaming, only to be awakened hours later by a loud, violent rush of air and a blast of light.

CHAPTER

11

BEFORE **I** KNEW WHAT WAS HAPPENING, I threw my hands up to protect myself from the brightness. I squeezed my eyes shut tight, not sure if I was asleep or awake. Stumbling to my feet, I shook off Pa's flannel. There were patches of light around me—a big one under the copper pot, and several smaller ones thrown about, flickering. I could make out Pa's form against the light. He was staggering toward me, then wrapped me up in his arms.

"To the creek," he mumbled.

"What happened?"

"To the creek."

Pa was half pushing me from behind, guarding me from the fires burning throughout the clearing. I felt his hands guiding me as we crashed through the woods. As soon as I could hear the stream gurgling ahead, Pa shoved me hard and I plunged into the water. He splashed down right next to me.

The night water was bitter cold, and I began scrambling to get out. I coughed and thrashed in the swirling water, finally pulling myself up onto the bank.

"Pa, what happened?" I yelled. "Is he here?" My voice was shaking.

"Are you burned?" he asked.

The moonlight was broken up by the pine needles above, but through the reflection off the water I could see my hands and arms, and they were all right. I ran my fingertips across my face and felt some raised scratches from the branches, but no burns.

"Did the still blow up?" I asked.

Pa was looking down at his palms and opening and closing his hands.

"Help me out of this shirt," was all he said.

"Pa!" I screamed.

His hands and arms were pale pink, the skin all bubbled. His charred shirtsleeves were falling off of him into the water.

"Just pull it over my head," he said.

I gently tried to lift the shirttail over his head, but it was wet and stuck against his back.

"Just pull. I'm all right."

I tugged and Pa grimaced, but we finally peeled the shirt off him. He fell backwards into the pool and sunk down with the water up to his chin. He closed his eyes and winced.

"You've got to put the fire out," he said, his eyes still shut. "I . . . I can't move."

I looked up to the clearing and saw flames crawling along the ground. I looked back at Pa, perfectly still in the water, breathing slow. I didn't budge.

"Go," he said. "Put the fire out." His eyes shot open and he added, "Don't touch the bucket."

I backed away slowly, then turned and dashed up to the clearing, guided by the scattered flames. I stomped on some big burning clumps of dried leaves and spotted the bucket in the distance, flames rising off it six feet tall. The side had caved in, but it was too big to step on.

"Pa!" I yelled. "The bucket's burning!"

I could hear his voice in the distance, but the words were lost. The copper pot on the still was scorched. The topper was in place and the condenser barrel was still connected. It had not exploded, but the metal was all black. The copper coil was still dripping shine into a big bottle, and I grabbed it using my shirtsleeves. I dumped the liquor out of it as I ran back to the creek.

Pa had not moved. I held the bottle underwater until no more air bubbles came up.

"You all right, Pa?"

"I'm fine."

I ran back up to the clearing, careful not to spill the water, and emptied the bottle over the bucket. The flames disappeared with a hiss, smoke burning my eyes. With all the fires out, I ran back to Pa sitting alone in the dark.

"Fire's out?" he asked.

"It's out. What happened?" I asked, panting. I still had no idea what had caused the fire.

"The bucket blew up."

"What?" I cried.

"I think it was full of gasoline."

This sent a shock through me that buckled my shoulders. It had not been an accident. Someone was trying to hurt Pa on purpose. I stood there paralyzed, hands clamped over my mouth.

"Cub," Pa said.

I jumped and looked down at him.

He spoke calmly. "Listen to me. Go get Yunsen. Tell him to bring his medicines."

I heard him but did not move. I couldn't.

"Go on. Take the lantern and bring him to the house. I'll be there."

"I'm staying with you," I said. The wind blew against my wet shirt and I started trembling.

"Go get him and meet me at the house. Please. Go."

The cold wind and Pa's words pulled me out of my shock, and I broke for the house. I ran past the edges of the cornfields, past Ma's grave and around the back of town toward Rebecca's house. I ran as hard as I could, cold, scared, and not once slowing from a dead sprint. I tried to hold the lantern in front of me, but the glass kept clanging against my wrists, and the flame sputtered out. I dropped it and ran harder, coming up on Rebecca's house so fast I nearly crashed through the front door.

I pounded on it, and Yunsen came out in a nightshirt. I tried to explain what happened, but I was gulping air so bad I couldn't talk. Soon enough, though, the two of us were in that big Buick, cutting through the darkness back to the house.

Pa was sitting calmly at the kitchen table. He had managed to get back home and light the kerosene lamp. He sat bare-chested, breathing slowly, waiting. Mr. Yunsen pulled him out of his seat and led him into the bedroom, where he set his black leather bag of materials at the foot of the bed and went to work.

"Bring a blanket for his shoulders," he said.

I rushed off to my room and brought back my red blanket.

"You bring remedies?" Pa asked.

Mr. Yunsen fiddled around in his bag, then shook his head. "I only work on the deceased. I have sutures and scalpels, but I'm afraid I'm ill-equipped for treating a burn."

"You don't have anything that can cure him?" I asked.

"Find me some honey," he said.

I ran to the kitchen and came back with the coffee can full of honey and honeycomb bits.

Mr. Yunsen smoothed the honey over the burns with his fingers, then pulled a clump of some yellow herb from his bag and gently pressed it into Pa's blistered skin.

"I do have a bit of dried elderflower," Mr. Yunsen said to me. "You're going to have to keep up the applications."

Except for Pa's arms, it looked like all the color had been drained right out of him.

He took a deep breath and said, "I had finished and fetched the bucket to put the fire out. As soon as I started pouring, I saw a flame run up like a lit fuse. The bucket blew up in my hands."

Mr. Yunsen's face turned severe. "You believe it to have been sabotage?"

Pa nodded. "Somebody put something flammable in the bucket."

"It does sound like gasoline," Mr. Yunsen said. "You couldn't smell it?"

"I didn't smell a thing. Just smoke from the fire," he said. "Could have been shine too, I reckon. You touch a flame to either one of 'em and they'll go up like gunpowder."

Pa turned to face me now and said, "Those flames were everywhere—covered both of us completely."

I only remembered the light.

"I can't believe you weren't hurt," Pa said, shaking his head.

"It was a blessing," Mr. Yunsen said.

I turned to Pa and said, "It was your flannel shirt."

One of Pa's arms was much worse than the other. Whereas pink patches and burned hair dotted his left arm, the meat of his right arm was a web of shiny red lines and murky yellow bubbles. Mr. Yunsen finished treating them both and wrapped his left one in cotton gauze, leaving the other to breathe. He showed me how to use the honey, cotton, and elderflower, then before leaving asked Pa one last time, "You're sure it wasn't an accident?"

"I'm sure," Pa said. He didn't look angry, only tired.

Pa and I were left sitting in the flickering lamplight in his room. His eyelids kept drooping, but I could tell he was fighting to work out what had happened. He had an uncommonly powerful mind when he could focus it. At that moment, he was bent on figuring out who the coward was who'd pulled the sneak attack and burned him. I had already solved the mystery. It was me.

CHAPTER 12

AS THE SPARROWS STARTED CHIRPING at dawn, I lugged my old mattress into Pa's room so I could keep watch over him. He had gone to sleep, and the only sound in the house was his slow breathing. I lay down on my mattress, watching a grass spider twist its web in the rafters and stewing in my own regret. Even as the guilt gnawed at my insides, I knew I had to clear my thinking and figure out what to do.

I was certain Mr. Salvatore had done this. Whether he was trying to kill Pa or just scare us I didn't know. Maybe he was trying to kill me too. Maybe he didn't care either way. We couldn't go to the police. The sheriff wasn't on our side. Nobody was.

The question was if Mr. Salvatore would come back. *Consolidating or eliminating.* Was he just trying to scare us into working for him? Or had he intended to murder us?

Late morning, I rose and made toast and coffee for Pa. The

thought of eating made my stomach turn, but Pa had to keep his energies up. I was standing there in the kitchen when I finally realized I was supposed to be in school.

For a second, I wanted nothing more than to be sitting there at my desk like the other kids. The thought surprised me, given how torturous I usually found the place, but I could not deny it. I took the plate and mug into Pa's room and woke him gently.

"Somebody here?" Pa asked, jerking straight up in bed.

"No, Pa. Take some food."

He ate slowly and peeled the wet bandage off to have a look at his left arm.

"I don't think I'll lose this one," he said through a mouthful of toast.

He pulled his other arm up and we studied the gleaming red burns circling it. He straightened it slowly, wincing as he tried not to crack the drying blisters.

"This one's . . . this one's a little worse," he said.

It should have been me, I thought, staring at his wounds. I wanted to look away but couldn't, like I had to pay a penance by looking at the red crocodile flesh.

When I finally broke my gaze, I found Pa staring at me. His eyes were almost as red as his arms.

"During the fire you said, 'Is he here?' Who were you talking about?"

I shook my head and looked away. "I don't recall saying that."

"No?" he asked, his voice a whisper.

"No, but . . . but I've been thinking about it. And I know what happened. It was an accident. We've been so busy these days working, and . . . shine and water must have somehow got mixed up."

His eyes were so big and red, and he wasn't blinking for some reason. It felt like he was looking right through me. Or right into my traitorous little mind.

"Except you didn't even touch the bucket last night. And for weeks it's been just me working. So that would mean I did it to myself."

"I . . . I think it was an accident," I stammered.

"I don't. And I know how to find out who did it too."

There was a sudden pressure in the room that was liable to collapse my lungs. I turned to face him, but he was leaning back in bed to rest. Sitting on my mattress, I hung my head so low it felt like my neck was going to snap.

All morning Pa dozed, and I kept watch out the window, just waiting for the end of the world to come rolling down the drive. I started to fall asleep only to catch Pa staring at the Winchester propped up in the corner, which made me wonder for a second if he thought he could shoot his way out of this. Next thing I knew, Pa was kicking at the mattress to wake me up.

"Car," he whispered.

I was up and at the window almost before my eyes opened. An automobile had turned up the drive, barreling toward us in the late afternoon sun.

"Is it Salvatore?" Pa asked. He was trying to tuck his knee-length nightshirt into his trousers. He stepped into his boots with no socks and started toward the window.

"No," I said. "It's the sheriff."

"I knew it," he growled.

I couldn't figure why the sheriff had come. Pa looked to understand things perfectly well because he went straight to the Winchester and racked a shell into the chamber.

"What are you doing?" I cried.

"Out the back door. Run."

"Pa, no!"

I grabbed for the gun barrel, but he twisted away.

He said, "The sheriff is the one who tried to kill me. I knew whoever showed up here first would be coming to make sure he'd finished the job. He's not getting another chance without a fight. You get out of here."

He pushed past me, and I flailed for the gun again, my fingers raking across his bandages. It must have hurt him, but he didn't falter and walked toward the door. Outside, I heard the police car door slam shut.

"It wasn't him!" I yelled. "It was Mr. Salvatore. I know it was."

Pa spun and was in my face before the last word was out. The gun was crossed over his chest, and I got one hand on the stock and one hand on the barrel. We stood there holding it between us.

"What?"

"I told him no," I stammered. "In town, I saw him. I told him you said no. That's why he didn't come. And why he—"

"You knew?" he yelled, ripping the shotgun out of my hands.

"No! I didn't know he was going to do that."

He stared at the floor, mouth slack, head shaking slightly.

A pounding on the front door made me jump. Pa looked like he hadn't even heard it.

"Jennings, you in there?" called Sheriff Bardo.

Slowly, Pa took his eyes off the floor and looked at me. His face didn't look like his own. And in turn, he looked at me like I was some stranger in his house, like we weren't blood anymore. My body chilled from the outside in, and I thought, He hates me.

The door rattled again as the sheriff banged on it.

"Jennings!"

Pa walked into his room, then returned without the gun and without looking at me. He opened the front door.

The sheriff had come alone and was standing nearly in the

doorframe. His eyes went straight to Pa's bandages, and he asked, "What happened to you?"

I reckon he caught sight of the pink flesh on the other arm because then he yelled out, "Good Lord!"

Pa ignored him and walked onto the porch. I followed, watching the sheriff's face. It almost looked like he was worried about Pa.

"You need a doctor," the sheriff said, pointing at Pa's arm.

"Did you do it?" Pa asked.

"Did I do what?"

"Did you do it?" he repeated through gritted teeth. He stuck both arms out and lifted his chin so the sheriff could see the rosy blister on his neck.

The sheriff's eyebrows squished together in disgust and confusion.

"Did your still blow?" he asked.

"I don't have a still," Pa said weakly. He didn't even try to lie well.

"Then what happened?" the sheriff asked.

"Somebody burned me."

The sheriff's eyes grew large and he shifted around from one leg to the other. I could tell he was trying to work it all out in his head. He squirmed under his big white cowboy hat, and like a bolt from the blue I saw my chance for redemption.

"You've got to arrest him," I said to the sheriff.

"Arrest who?"

"Salvatore. He did this," I said. "Arrest him."

The sheriff paused for a second, then frowned.

"Maybe I should arrest the two of you for shining."

I stared at the sheriff's puckered face and for the first time was hit with the enormity of what I had done. The sheriff would not take him to jail. He was in Salvatore's pocket. As were Pa and I. Everything was worse because of me, and we had no way out.

"Why'd you come here anyways?" Pa asked.

I saw the sheriff glance at Pa's blistered arm again, then look away.

"To tell you to change your danged mind, Earl. They told me you were causing problems, and that means problems for me. You could have kept shining, and none of this would have happened. These aren't men to be messed with. And . . . well, now this," he said, pointing at Pa's burns.

Voice quaking, I yelled, "Then why'd you come here telling us to stop shining in the first place? Saying you were gonna take us to jail?"

The sheriff jumped back a bit, startled by my outburst. He leaned forward and answered in a hushed voice, like we weren't the only three people within miles.

"They wanted control of the liquor business. Complete control. Anyone not working for them had to go, they said. So I told you to stop. But then they saw how much they were selling up North and needed more. Always more, more, more. So I sent them to you."

I noticed the sheriff had still not said Salvatore's name, and instead referred to him as "they," which was troubling.

The sheriff shook his finger at Pa. "I was doing you a favor, Earl. How stupid can you be to say no?"

Seeing him insult my pa like that made me feel more shamefaced than I'd thought possible. I had to tell him that I was the one who'd said no. That it was me who could be that stupid. I started to open my mouth, but Pa put his hand on the back of my neck and gave me a squeeze that told me to be quiet.

The sheriff spat on our porch and walked back down toward his car.

"Stupid," the sheriff repeated, and as he said it Pa looked down at me and squeezed my neck again. I winced and felt his hand fall away.

The sheriff got back into his car and drove away. When the dust trail had faded, I said, "I was going to own up to it."

"You don't say a word about that, you hear me?" he snapped.

Pa seldom raised his voice at me, and it stung.

"But why not?"

"Don't you know anything? You get any more mixed up in this and you'll get yourself killed. What do you think a gangster is going to do to some punk kid screwing with his business?"

I gritted my teeth, angry and embarrassed. Pa leaned down and poked his finger into my chest.

"You get it now? He would kill you. I am not the problem. *You* are the problem."

CHAPTER 13

I STORMED INTO MY ROOM ready to throw myself down onto my mattress, only to realize I'd left it in Pa's room. That made me even madder and all I felt was an overwhelming urge to break something. My room was empty save for the two drawers on the floor, so I kicked one as hard as I could. It went end over end into the wall, the flimsy wood splitting with a crack and dumping my shirts onto the floor.

"You ain't done enough damage already?" Pa said from behind me.

I shoved past him without a thought for his burns. Before I had any idea of what I was doing, I was out the back door and running down the path into the woods.

The sun was going down and the few rays that cut through the brush were pushing my shadows east, so I followed them with no plan. I just watched my boots stomping down on my shadow.

By the time I stopped, now shivering and shaking, I was

standing on the sandy edge of Copperhead Creek on the far side of town. What was usually just a little trickle had swollen into a rush of dark waters, almost a river. The sun had set, and I just stared and listened to the creek's flow hit the rocks. For a moment I thought about throwing myself in and seeing where I wound up. But as I gazed into the gloomy water, I realized I had nowhere to go but home. That house that had been my whole world now seemed so little it would suffocate me as soon as I stepped inside it and saw Pa.

I stuck my hands into the pockets of my denims and braced against the wind, following the creek north back to town. Near Elm I stopped and looked at the schoolhouse, all mysterious and unfamiliar-looking in the night, and I wondered if I could get in through a window and sleep there. I kept walking in the moonlight and reached the turn to Rebecca's house, but didn't even think about going there. She had no idea of the criminal things I was mixed up in, and if I told her then she'd probably never speak to me again.

Main Street was empty except for a fancy-dressed couple coming out of a picture show and a drunk sitting against the wall of Beckwith Methodist. My foot was aching from kicking the drawer, and I stumbled on for miles until I finally reached our drive. There were no cars there, but the kerosene lamp shone in the front window.

I had used the time out of the house to get my words together in my head.

I walked in and looked dead at Pa as he jumped up from the kitchen table.

"You nearly scared the life outta me! Where have you been?"

"I messed up, and I'm sorry. But I didn't want to work for a criminal, and I didn't want you to either. And now you see why not," I said, nodding at his burns.

His face hardened.

"That wasn't your decision to make. It was my decision."

"I thought we were partners," I said.

"You're no partner of mine," he said. "Just a boy who doesn't do what his father tells him."

I stumbled back a half step, like he'd pushed me.

Right when I was about to say something back, I caught the lamplight reflecting on that wet pink burn on his neck, and I stopped. He looked so saddened by me. And I could see in his eyes he didn't h ave a clue how to make things right. And I didn't either. His little miracle boy had gotten him into this mess and now wasn't smart enough to get him out of it.

Shaking my head, I turned on him and dragged my mattress out of his room and into mine. I threw it on the ground with a loud whump, then threw myself on top of it. There was no creaking of the floorboards in the kitchen so I knew Pa was still just standing there, that broken look in his eyes. I punched the mattress twice and lay there until I was asleep.

The draft from the corner woke me early, and I was confused for a second why I still had my denims on. The house was silent, and I peeked into Pa's room without him seeing me. He was there with no shirt on, trying to unstick his open wounds from the bedsheet. Looking at the clear, jelling ooze on his arm, I thought I might be sick. He had to be feeling a thousand times worse.

With a sigh, I went in. "I'll get it."

I tried to separate his arm from the sheet, but it was like they'd been glued together. Pulling the sheet tight, the skin finally popped loose, leaving a wet pink blotch on the fabric.

"I could have done it," Pa said, his voice soulless.

I went into the kitchen and heated the can of honey to soften it up. I took it back in with the cotton and herbs. I could at least try to keep him from getting infected.

"What's going to happen now, Pa?" I asked.

I stuck the wooden spoon into the honey, accidentally crushing a chunk of honeycomb.

"If I tell you, can you keep your mouth shut about it?"

One of my best abilities had always been keeping quiet. It was a moonshiner essential. Apparently I didn't have it anymore.

"Just tell me."

"Last night while you were gone, I had a fellow over to the house, a horse skinner who did time in El Paso. He knows about these kinds of things. I gave him some liquor, and he told me what he knew."

"And?"

"Salvatore really is with some big gang from up North."

Gang. My head went wobbly like when I'd drunk the shine. Pa went on talking while I tried to stop the room from tilting.

"But he said he'd get Salvatore to come back on Friday."

"What?" I cried, accidentally mashing the spoon into Pa's raw flesh.

"Ow! Dang it, Cub, be careful."

"We got to get out of here! That's tomorrow."

"Just calm yourself. I'm going to tell him I was mistaken, but that now I'd be grateful to work for him."

I didn't say anything, just smeared the honey around on his arm without even looking at what I was doing. Grateful to work for him? Those didn't sound like Pa's words. I'd thought I was being a big man marching up to Salvatore and telling him no. Now begging to work for him was the closest we could get to being safe. In what kind of upside-down world was Pa meeting with a killer who'd lit him on fire a step in the right direction?

"I just hope the price he gives me is enough for us to survive off of," Pa said.

"Maybe you could wear your negotiating shoes?" I offered with a smile.

"They're bad luck," he said, then looked at me. "Everything is."

I didn't know what was worse—the situation we were in or the guilt I was saddled with for trying to think for myself and ruining everything. They were twisted tight around each other like creeper vines, but maybe if I could get rid of one, the other would fall away. I pressed the elderflower buds hard into Pa's sores.

"We've got to get out of this, Pa. Out of shining, away from Mr. Salvatore, away from all this."

I braced myself for the explosion, but when I looked up, his face bore that same look of defeat and detachment.

Quietly he said, "If I'd have known how bad this was going to get, I'd have found some new trade back when the getting was good. But you know since the crash, there ain't no jobs. And without us shining, there ain't no food."

That was true. We didn't have any money. We couldn't move away. We didn't have any family outside this dusty shack we were holed up in. We had a tiny patch of corn, a shotgun, and an oak tree full of illegal liquor.

"Mr. Salvatore's coming tomorrow?" I asked.

"Yeah. So after school you go to Mr. Yunsen's house and wait for me there."

"I'm not going to school."

"You have to," Pa said, his eyes looking sad. "It's safer there."

"I'll be fine here."

He scoffed and said, "Having you there is safer for *both* of us."

He didn't want me around. Maybe he'd be happier if I was in the orphanage. Everything was crumbling.

"But what are you going to tell him?" I asked.

"I'll tell him I'm going to work for him and that's it."

I exhaled slowly, considering it. There were no other options.

"You don't think he'll do anything crazy, do you?"

"Not as long as he's getting his way."

Terrific. We'd gone from shining for food money to working for a gangster who'd have no problem having his own St. Valentine's Day Massacre on us right there in our house.

CHAPTER

14

FROM THE SECOND **I** WALKED into the schoolroom the next morning, I could feel Miss Pounder eyeballing me. I tried to smile at her, but it came out more like a quiver, and I just headed for my stump. The past two days had me feeling beat up, and I still had to worry about Mr. Salvatore coming to the house today.

Miss Pounder waited until I'd sat down before she called me to her desk. I marched back up. Everybody in there was watching me now and waiting for a show.

"Cub, you were absent yesterday."

"Um, I'm sorry."

I heard the whole class laugh behind me. Miss Pounder shook her head.

"You don't have to be sorry. You just have to give me a note."

"Yes, Miss Pounder," I said, and started walking back to my seat.

"Where are you going?" she asked, above the class's giggles.

I wheeled around and threw my hands up. "To write you your note!"

The class was boiling over with laughter now. I'd done it again.

"From a parent, Cub. You have to bring a note explaining your absence," she said.

"I didn't know, all right?" I said, ten times louder than necessary. "There was no way for me to know."

I'd just yelled at every person in the class. Miss Pounder's mouth was hanging open. Everybody else gaped at me like I was on the verge of going completely nuts, which I was. Looking up and down the rows of desks, I glared at them, challenging someone to tell me how I could have known. When they didn't, I slumped into my desk.

At lunch Rebecca and I sat outside on an old cedar bench, Rebecca swinging her legs, me staring at the ground. Rebecca didn't seem to know I'd been at her house the other night, or about what had happened to Pa. Mr. Yunsen must have kept quiet about it.

She had a bean sandwich and was nice enough to share with me because I had forgotten to bring a lunch. I had two bites, but my guts were so twisted up I felt like I was about to turn inside out.

"Grandpa said you were coming over today. Told me not to let you escape," she said with a giggle.

"Did he say anything else?" I asked.

"About what?"

I shook my head and said, "I'd like to go to your house today. But I can't."

I wasn't going to leave Pa alone at the house. I'd already decided that. And he'd be furious at me for it. But I didn't care if he put me in the orphanage himself later or packed me on a ship to China, I was going to try to help him.

"Grandpa said . . ."

"I know, and I'm sorry."

She shook her head. "Tell me why not or I'm gonna drag you to my house by your hair."

Not knowing too many folks had always made it easy for me to keep my mouth shut about shining. And keeping the secret had made it special for me and Pa. It was our little trick on the world. But at that moment, I felt like I had the pressure of the still inside me, the boiler cap ready to blow right off.

"If I tell you something, you can't tell anybody. Nobody at school, no teachers, nobody."

Rebecca leaned in, obviously excited. "Of course."

I took a deep breath, then let it out. "Me and my pa make moonshine. It's a kind of alcohol and it's against the law."

"I know what it is. My grandpa used to sell it."

"We got mixed up with someone bad. A crook. Maybe worse. He burned my pa."

Her eyes grew wide. "Did the doctor go see him?"

"No. Your grandpa took care of him. It was the middle of the night."

"What?" she asked. "Grandpa? When?"

"Two nights ago. But my pa's okay."

"Why didn't you tell me?" she asked.

I had no answer and waited for her to fly off the handle at me. Involving her grandpa involved her, and she had a right to be mad.

"Did you tell the police at least?" she asked finally.

"They already know. The sheriff knows the man who did it. But he won't do anything."

"That's ridiculous," she said, and shook her head. "No, no. I'm sure he will. The sheriff has to. It's what he does."

"That's what I always thought too. But when you're doing crimes, nobody has to help you."

Rebecca turned toward me and grabbed my arm.

"There's always somebody, Cub. Like whoever is higher than the sheriff."

"Who, like the chief of police? Maybe the president? I should just write to Hoover, huh?"

She squeezed my arm hard. "It's not just the two of you out there on your little farm. People can help you. I can help you."

We looked at each other and I didn't see the tough girl slapping people across the back of the head. I saw someone who understood about losing your family.

"Yeah, but how?"

She let go of my arm.

"I could let you go to your house today, for one."

After school let out, I raced home, half hoping I could make it in time and half terrified of what I'd find there. I skirted around our eastern field and saw an automobile and two people standing on the porch, one person in a slick suit, the other with his arms bandaged so much they looked like two cotton puffs sticking out from his body.

They hadn't seen me yet and I had next to no plan of what I was going to do or say, so I slowed to a jog and headed up to them.

Pa spotted me coming up the drive and his whole body went rigid.

As soon as I was in earshot, he yelled, "Cub, you get out of here. I'm doing business."

Salvatore turned and looked at me, lips curling into an ugly smile.

I didn't stop. Pa stepped down off the porch, like he was blocking me out. I walked up until we were face-to-face.

"This is my house too, isn't it?" I asked.

"Let the boy stay," Salvatore said from the porch. "He needs to learn a lesson too."

He was looking down on both of us, like he had taken over.

Pa exhaled loudly and said, "I think we were about finished anyway."

"Tell your boy the deal," Salvatore said. "Because he didn't understand things too well last time," he added with a smirk.

Pa said, "Two deliveries a month, a hundred gallons each time."

"Two hundred gallons a month?" I asked, sure I'd misheard. When it had been the both of us working every night, two hundred gallons would have been tough. With Pa's arms almost useless and me in school all day, it would be about three steps past impossible. Once the stash in the tree ran out, I'd probably have to quit school and work day and night at the still.

Pa said nothing. He knew what a raw deal it was. I didn't dare ask about the money. Salvatore clomped down the stairs, pushing his way right between me and Pa.

"See you soon," he said as he climbed into his automobile.

Pa and I stood rooted in the dirt and watched him speed off.

"Two hundred gallons can't be done, Pa."

"I told you to go to Yunsen's after school," he said quietly.

I'd expected him to blow up on me when Salvatore left.

"I'm sorry," I said, head down. "I just wanted to help."

"My fault, too, I reckon. I shouldn't have expected you to do anything right."

That stung more than any yelling could have.

"I'm gonna help, Pa. You'll see. But two hundred gallons—"

"We'll just work and that'll be the end of it," Pa said.

He was talking about our future like we were dead and buried already.

"I'll work as much as I can."

He just shrugged and headed off down the drive.

"Where you going?"

I had a thought he was just going to walk off and never come back.

Over his shoulder he said, "Gotta trade for some sugar."

"Can I go with you?"

He stopped and turned back, finally looking at me.

"Does it matter if I say yes or no?"

We trudged into town in silence, and I didn't say a word as he made a deal with Mr. Willis in the back room of the general store. The big burlap sacks of sugar would arrive tomorrow. We'd start working as soon as they did, then likely never stop.

We started back, but near Elm Street I realized the last place I wanted to go right then was home, and I imagined Pa felt the same.

"Pa, you never took me to the place you and Ma lived at. I'd like to see it."

He turned and squinted at me, confused. "You want to go now?"

I nodded.

"It ain't far from here. Turn left past the McMillan place," he said, then kept heading toward our place.

"Ain't you coming?" I called.

Ten yards away, he turned and shook his head.

"Last thing I need now is more bad memories. You go on."

"Maybe it'd do you good. Remind you of your life before me."

He stared at me for a long moment, then threw up his hands in a blast-it-all kind of way.

"Well, you don't have to be so danged dramatic about it," he said as we walked toward the McMillan place.

I was relieved to be going somewhere no criminals or lawmen could find us, even if only for a short while.

CHAPTER

15

AS THE CROW FLIES, THE FARM could not have been more than half a mile from Rebecca's house, and I'd probably passed by there a hundred times without thinking twice. It was a simple white house, one level and sturdy, and not in terrible shape, but clearly abandoned. The windows had been boarded up with scrap wood to keep vagrants out, and the white paint was peeling off into little curls that dropped and hung in the surrounding crabgrass. Clover overran the front yard, and knotweed shoots poked up through the slats in the porch floorboards. The whole place was in terrible need of some fixing up, and I could feel Pa's disappointment.

"Looks nice, Pa."

"Used to look a lot nicer."

We walked first toward the fields, where little dust devils swirled around the withered cornstalks. It looked like nothing had been planted for years. Crows and field mice had picked out everything they could eat seasons ago.

"How big is it, Pa?"

"Hundred and ninety-four acres," he said, looking out over his old fields. A proudness came into his voice, something I hadn't heard since the attack. He sounded almost alive again.

"How come there's nobody here?" I asked.

"Money troubles, I reckon. Seems to be a lot of that going around. I'd bet you the bank owns it now, or the government."

Pa stubbed the toe of his boot under a clod of dirt, then kicked harder.

"Look at that," he said.

I squatted down to have a look. Beneath a fine layer of dust were rich black crumbles. I rubbed the dirt in my hand. It was moist and stained my fingertips.

"There's an underground spring. Keeps the dirt wet and the pond full," Pa said.

We crossed through the weeds toward the east side of the house. I spied a busted window with a board missing and peeked in. It was the kitchen—empty save for about two inches of dust on the floor. I tried to picture my ma walking around in there, cooking up corn bread or something, but all I could imagine was a faceless woman doing all that.

Together we headed down a slight hill behind the house, and not more than fifty yards away I caught the shine of sun on water. It was an oval-shaped pond, a whole lot bigger than I'd imagined. The water looked as clear as what we pumped out of the well at home. As I walked down to the edge, a shadowy shape beneath the surface darted away.

"A fish! I saw a fish!"

"Bass and bluegills," Pa said quietly.

"And you never come here to fish?" I asked. I'd never known Pa to pass up a good fishing hole.

"Never could bring myself to come back out here," he said, staring out at the water. "I reckon you could if you wanted. Just don't let nobody see you."

I thought on it for a second, but decided it wouldn't be much fun without Pa. The place had a feeling to it like it was more for a family, not just one person.

We walked a quarter of the pond's edge and sat on a limbless log. The wind was blowing ripples toward us, and I could see a mallard flying circles on the horizon, probably scared to land because of us. I had a crab apple I'd found near school and carved out a thick piece with my pocketknife for Pa. He chomped on it and stretched out his legs and settled into the log. He didn't want to go home either, I reckoned.

He said, "I tell you I wouldn't mind having this place again. I could have that corn shooting out of the ground like we'd struck oil."

That spark was back in his voice, and I seized on it.

"Maybe you could get it, Pa. Ain't nobody living here now."

Pa blew out a breath and shook his head.

"We don't have any money, Cub. You know that."

I didn't say anything.

"You surprised me by wanting to come here," he said.

Who wouldn't want to come here?, I thought. It was even better than I'd imagined. Near town, near Rebecca's, a normal house. Not just a place to sleep when we weren't working the still out back.

"Sounded like a good place," I said.

"It was once. Me and your ma had a good life here."

"Before shining."

"Before your ma got sick," he said sharply. "And before the government tried to take you away from me. I did what I had to do." He crunched his apple chunk loudly to make his point.

111

I wiped the knife blade across the knee of my overalls and flicked it shut. He had done what he had to do back then on account of me. All these years I'd been thinking I was doing him a favor helping with the business, when the whole danged operation was actually something he had been forced to throw together to take care of me. Then when he had finally found a way to do it without risking jail, I had butted in and almost gotten him killed.

I looked over and he was stock-still staring into the water, eyes wet from the wind. There was nothing I wanted more than to make things up to him.

We were silent passing through town on the way home, and I saw folks eyeing Pa's bandages under the cuff of his coat. Maybe they'd heard stories. Maybe Shane's preacher pa had been telling them.

As soon as we were home I walked right back out the door to see if I could find dinner. We hadn't sold a drop of shine in over a week and had no food at the house.

With about an hour of sunlight left, I headed west with Pa's Winchester over my shoulder and four shotgun shells in the chest pocket of my overalls. I had on what I'd started thinking of as me and Pa's lucky red flannel shirt. I just hoped it wouldn't bunch up and hurt my aim if I had to shoulder the gun fast.

A noisy pair of meadowlarks squawked at me from a fallen limb, but I walked on. I'd learned long ago not to waste a shot on anything that wouldn't make a decent meal. Or as Pa would say, "Don't shoot unless you're going to eat it or it's going to eat you."

I'd seen a few black bears before, but usually higher up in the hills. Still, they'd be getting ready to hibernate now and looking to fatten up on any meal they could find. And we'd had so many unexpected visitors lately a bear wouldn't have even surprised me then.

At the back end of the cornfield I walked up slowly on the gravesite. I didn't sit, just stood there with the gun in front of me, barrel to the sky.

"I thought I was doing something smart for once, but he got burned. I should have just listened to Pa, but . . . Well, you know what I did."

I shifted from foot to foot, unsure of what else to say. When the words came they were a surprise, like they'd come out of some part of me I didn't know was there.

"For so long it was just me and him. But now I know some other folks, and I've been seeing there are other ways of doing things. Ways that don't land you in jail or an orphanage or burned up. He thinks working for Salvatore is our only option now. I don't. But I don't know what else to do."

I bowed slightly, then walked north. The nights were coming sooner now, with the sun dropping behind the western cornfields early and no more lightning bugs around. I reached a patch of sumac where I knew rabbits holed up, and I stomped through, brushing my pant leg against each bush in hopes of spooking something out.

A fluttering caught my eye, and I spun, ready to shoot, but it was just a magpie flailing about on a cedar branch. He looked injured, maybe winged by buckshot, but then I saw he didn't have his tail feathers yet and figured he was still a baby. Sure enough there was a nest of barnyard grass wedged in the cedar's crook and a big mama bird standing guard.

She kept slapping at the baby with her big black-and-white wings, and I was thinking she was pretty abusive before I realized she was trying to get him to fly down to eat some of the black beetles below. They were teeming out of a hole in a rotten log, and beetle was a fine meal for a magpie, but the baby had his little bird mind set against it. The mother finally smacked him off the limb, and he flew down as graceful as any eagle, then crash-landed beak-first into the dirt. He collected himself and started feeding, and it reminded me I didn't have food yet myself, so I walked on.

Zigzagging from shrub to shrub, I fell into deep thinking. Pa had said it himself—without shining we'd starve. And now with Salvatore around, if we didn't shine we'd be dead too, but gangster style.

But what about Mr. Salvatore? I didn't know. Not yet. There were so many questions, and I was sick of Pa's answers. Was there somebody else I could talk to?

There was a rustle in the brush next to me, and a streak of gray jolted me out of my thoughts. A giant hare was bounding away, its massive hind legs coming up behind its ears as it dashed off. I dropped to a knee and threw the gun up to my shoulder. Aiming a yard ahead of the hare, I squeezed the trigger. The mass of fur flipped once, then stopped.

"Whoo!" I ran over and grabbed the hare by its giant back feet. One shot, killed instantly. And it was big. I held it up by its back legs, and the hare's front paws nearly dragged on the ground. It was three times the size of a cottontail.

I had our supper, food for tomorrow, and maybe even enough to share with Rebecca. I'd gotten something big in one shot. Maybe that was the key to everything.

CHAPTER 16

THE NEXT DAY AT LUNCH, Rebecca and I sat under the school's one maple tree, sharing our food and making a stick corral for a pair of ladybugs we'd found. The night before, I'd cooked the rabbit in butter and pepper and saved a big piece in wax paper. I had a bite of Rebecca's ham sandwich as well, to make it more like a trade.

"You think maybe I could go to your house today?" I asked.

"Nope. Yesterday you were invited and said no. I was even going to show you the secret basement. Folks used to hide there during President Lincoln's war."

"It was an emergency. But can I? I was hoping I could talk to your grandpa."

She brought the rabbit leg down from her mouth and wiped the butter off her chin with the back of her hand. "What for?"

"I'm trying to help my pa. And your grandpa knows a lot, maybe he could help me."

She kept staring at me, her eyes squinting so tight they almost closed. "Grandpa used to do crazy stuff, but not anymore."

"I just want to talk to him."

She kept on staring at me, and I figured it was hopeless. She raised her finger and pointed it at me, then cocked her head to the side in warning.

"You're lucky this rabbit is so good. You can talk to him."

After school that afternoon, Mr. Yunsen and I sat at the dining room table in Rebecca's house, me with a piece of paper and the nub of a pencil in front of me, Mr. Yunsen with his hands crossed casually before him.

"I had understood we were meeting yesterday, Cub."

I nodded apologetically and said, "Things changed."

That could sum up my year.

"Why isn't your father here?"

"Um, this meeting was my idea."

Mr. Yunsen nodded.

When I was hunting yesterday, I would've had to shoot three rabbits to get the same amount of meat I got off that hare. It would have taken longer to find them all, and I'd have used two more shotgun shells. Instead, I'd just needed one shot for big results. That's how I was going to tackle our problem.

"Sir, me and my pa are in a bad scrape. But I was thinking maybe we could make one more big sale and then leave moonshining for good."

Mr. Yunsen sighed and began rolling up the cuffs on his shirt, revealing a web of purplish veins running up his chalk-white arms. You could almost see right through his skin.

"Cub, the incident with this Salvatore fellow is absolutely horrific, there's no question. And your eagerness to help your father is noble.

116

But I don't think this 'one more big sale' will help your situation or your relations with Salvatore at all. Quite the opposite."

This was true. A sale that did not go to Salvatore would be the death of us. If Salvatore was still around.

"I'm not looking at him as the problem. I'm looking at moonshining as the problem."

Mr. Yunsen drummed his fingers on the table and studied me.

"Interesting. Your decision to disregard this mobster is certainly daring. Foolhardy it would seem, but your approach is refreshing."

"I'm working on a plan for Mr. Salvatore."

Mr. Yunsen cocked a white eyebrow at me, waiting for me to explain.

"I haven't got the specifics nailed down just yet . . ."

His eyebrow dropped, and I sensed that his hopes for me and my pa came crashing down then too.

"It's just that I think me and my pa could get out of moonshining for good if we just had the money to get started on something new. I'm real good with numbers. If I knew the prices and whatnot, then I could count everything we've got stored and see if we have a chance."

"Prices? Well, I don't suppose there's any harm in sharing what I know. Provided that you are upfront with your father about our discussion."

We talked for almost two hours. Rebecca had obviously inherited her talking skills from her grandpa. And that old man knew all there was to know about moonshining, rum-running, bootlegging— plumb near everything that had to do with selling illegal liquor. And he'd heard more rumors about Mr. Salvatore and his crew, who were spreading like termites throughout the state.

Police had been bribed, terrorized, and corrupted, and no one had been able to escape their control. Every drop of alcohol was being shipped up North and local prices were through the roof.

On my paper I scribbled prices, town names, amounts of shine, everything I could.

I thanked Mr. Yunsen after the meeting, then thanked Rebecca, who appeared at the bottom of the giant wooden staircase and eyed me suspiciously. I headed home with half the numbers I needed. The other half I got counting our stocks in the tree.

The night's dew had already coated the grass by the time I reached the house, and as soon as the back door creaked open, Pa pounced on me.

"Where have you been?" he yelled, jumping out of his chair.

I took a step back.

"I was at Rebecca's," I said. "I didn't know I was going until today."

"Don't you do that without telling me! I nearly had a fit sitting here wondering where you were. I thought you'd gotten into it with somebody."

I stared back at him.

"I didn't."

I started to head past him, but he stepped right in front of me. Leaning down in my face, he said, "Don't you go anywhere without telling me. School and come home, that's it for you."

I had gone to school, then I'd started working on how to save us. He'd been sitting at the house all day.

"Why should I listen to you?"

Pa's eyes blazed in the lamplight, and I saw him swallow hard, like he'd just choked down something venomous instead of spitting it out at me. His legs were trembling, rattling the floorboards. Any peace we'd found between us at the farm yesterday was gone like smoke in the wind. I turned my back on him and went to my room to wait out the hours until supper.

We didn't speak all evening, and that silence, added to my desire to tell Pa my plan, was putting me into a frenzy. I walked circles in my room, stepping over pieces of the broken drawer and wishing I hadn't gotten him riled up. Pa barked at me to come eat, and as I sat at the table listening to him angrily chomp his navy beans, I asked, "Can I come with you to work tonight?"

Pa stopped chewing and stared at me like I'd asked to burn the house down, then swallowed in a big dry gulp. "Oh you're coming all right. I'm not going to be the only one breaking my back working out there. Now, if we'd gotten the original price I could hire a hand. But somebody told him no, so now we're glorified servants."

"That's what I want to talk to you about."

"Spit it out! You make your own hours now, do whatever you please. I'd say you're grown enough to say what's on your mind."

I looked down at the table. He wouldn't hear me out now. In the clearing, he'd be more open to talking.

After I'd cleaned the dinner plates, I followed him out into the woods. As I worked in the fire-lit shadows there, I watched him and his injured hands fumble with the tasks he had once done so easily. Striking a single match was near impossible for him, and despite my offers to help, Pa refused to take charity and wasted a good two dozen matches before the fire caught.

I tried to pretend it was just another night shining, like the ones we'd enjoyed for so many years. It wouldn't take. Even the smoke off the fire smelled more like a memory than anything real. In my gut, I knew I'd never enjoy shining again.

"Pa, I'm working on a plan."

He was using his fingers to spread red clay against a crack in one of the still's pipes. He stopped and waited.

"If we sell all the shine we got, maybe we would have enough money to get out of the business."

He looked at me and moved his cheeks back and forth like he was swishing the idea around in his mouth. I bit my lip and waited.

Finally he said, "What is it, boy? You want Salvatore to drown me too? Shoot me with a bow and arrow? Put wires in my ears and electrocute me? We can't get out now."

I kicked a stray log back into the fire. "But it would be a lot of money. And we need to get out."

Pa sighed and rubbed a sooty hand across his eyes, leaving a dark streak across his face like a raccoon.

"Look, I understand what you're trying to do. And if we sold all the shine we've got, we would have some money for a while. But only for a while. Then what?"

"Then maybe we could get that white house. We could just farm," I said quietly.

Pa walked around the condenser barrel, dragging a sharp stick across the ground.

"It's a nice idea. And I know you want to help."

He let out a bitter chuckle and held up his bandaged arm. "But the last thing I want right now is more of your help."

Here I was trying to do something and all he wanted to do was make me feel rotten.

"But you haven't even considered it," I said.

"And you haven't even considered the fact that I sold that place once. This is thousands of dollars we're talking. If I shined for ten years, we wouldn't have enough for it!" He flipped the stick end over end into the dirt, where it stuck and shuddered like an arrow.

"I counted everything we've got in the tree," I said.

"You did?"

"And I talked to Mr. Yunsen."

The firelight reflected off Pa's eyes as they grew wide. "What for?"

"To see about prices. He says we could get almost three times the price we usually get. Prices are sky-high because nobody's stood up to Salvatore."

I caught the spark from the fire in Pa's eye, and for a second I thought that the last part had triggered something in him.

"And you'd get some money if you sold this place too. Maybe you could even do a trade for the white house."

"This place ain't worth a quarter of that other one," Pa said with a scoff.

"But what about with this place, all the money from the shine in the tree, and you sell the still? Scrap the copper?"

I had gone in all or nothing. Sell the shine, sell the still, sell it all. And the still would bring a good sum of money, but its real value was something different. No still meant never moonshining again. Pa stared into the fire, shaking his head.

"What exactly do you think old Salvatore would say if I told him, 'Thanks, but I retired'? You tried telling him no once, remember?"

Rebecca had been the only one with a possible solution, so I threw it out there. "We'd have to get him in trouble," I said.

Pa turned and sputtered, "In trouble with who? His buddy the sheriff?"

"What about the government? Somebody higher up than the sheriff. If he's as bad as he seems, I bet they'd want to get him."

"What, like the Feds?"

I nodded. "Exactly!"

Pa responded with equal energy, but not the kind I had hoped for. "Nobody wants to help us. We've been breaking the law for ten years!" he yelled.

I remembered I'd said almost exactly the same thing to Rebecca. "Maybe they would, Pa. Somebody."

There was a whole world of people out there. I'd seen it myself now.

He glared at me. "Maybe you ought to go back to the house."

"This is no good, Pa, none of this. And I'm not just gonna sit around waiting for more trouble to come down on our heads."

He stood just two feet away, staring into the fire, but he could have been two towns over. I knew the talk was finished. I turned and started winding my way back toward the house. It had not gone like I'd hoped, not even close. But as I pushed through the damp pine needles, I felt a spark of pride inside. As I crossed on through the night, I thought that whatever happened now, at least I'd told him what I thought.

CHAPTER

17

THAT NEXT MORNING, I made the walk to school, glad to have an escape from Pa's pigheadedness. School was a good place to think, and even if I was still an outcast there, I did have Rebecca.

I reached the schoolyard a little early that day and found her sitting on a bench with a pair of girls I didn't know from the older class.

"How's your pa doing?" Rebecca asked.

I froze. The two older girls seemed to pick up on my unease and stared at me as I stood there dumb.

"Um, he's fine."

Rebecca said, "Cub, I got to confess something to you."

The two girls started giggling. One of them made kissy noises.

Rebecca elbowed her and said, "Oh, stop it, Francine."

I stood there, awkward as ever. Rebecca hopped off the bench and started walking me away from everyone, toward the maple tree.

That of course sent Francine and her friend into a fit.

"Cub, so I maybe did something that wasn't so honest. I might have done a little spying."

I waited, and then the words just came pouring out of her.

"But this whole business about Salvatore and the gangsters and making moonshine sales and running from the law is so danged interesting that once I started listening I just couldn't stop!"

Hearing her say the name "Salvatore" jarred me. My life had two sides now, and I didn't want them to touch. And Rebecca was here trying to mix water and oil, and at school, no less, where the whole world could hear.

Off behind me, Miss Pounder started clanging on the school bell and I almost jumped out of my boots. I glanced over my shoulder. People were heading inside. No one seemed to be paying us any attention, but my heart felt like it was about to thump out of my chest. I should have been mad at Rebecca for "listening," but all I wanted was for her to be quiet.

"Let's not talk about it here, okay?"

"Yeah, yeah, but it's just so crazy! It's like they're filming a gangster movie, and you're in it."

I shook my head hard and threw a finger to my lips.

"Heck, you're the star!" she said.

"Look, I'll explain it later, but I'm begging you just not to talk about it here. Making moonshine was something we had to do. We're not criminals."

"The heck you aren't!" Shane bellowed, storming out from behind the maple tree. "Ooh, I knew you were trash, and now I heard it from your own mouth. I got the evidence now!"

A chill ran down my arms, and I stared at his smirking face, wondering how much he had heard.

Rebecca scoffed. "What do you care anyways, Shane?"

No, no, no, I thought. Deny it. Say it was a joke.

Shane said, "My pa himself gave a sermon about how good families have to stick together against bad ones. And now I got a confession."

"My family's not bad," I muttered, but he just kept grinning at me, smug as could be.

From the school door, Miss Pounder yelled for the three of us to get inside.

"Yes, ma'am," Shane called out, then jogged in. In a daze, I made my way in and to our class. Rebecca walked with me and said something, but I was in such a state of fright I couldn't even hear what she was saying.

I watched the gossip begin to spread during first period. Shane turned around at his desk and told Jackson, who sneered at me from across the room. Jackson told Martha, who told the Bowery twins. By recess, I was positive that every student in both classes had heard me and Pa were moonshiners, and I gave it about a fifty-fifty chance the teachers now knew as well. As I trudged back in for arithmetic, I half expected Pounder to be waiting for me with handcuffs. As I headed to my stump, I caught words like "Mafia," "gangster," and "killer" in the classroom buzz. The whole lesson, all eyes were on me, but I just kept my gaze glued to the blackboard.

At lunch I tried to find Rebecca outside but was swarmed by Russ and his friends.

"Cub, is it true your pa is wanted by the cops?"

"How many guns do you guys have?"

"Are the coppers going to put your pa back in the big house?"

I shook my head and pushed past. Rebecca wasn't around, and I ended up sitting alone at the edge of the pines, alternating soggy bites of a cheese sandwich with bites of my fingernails, fuming in the shadows.

I'd told Rebecca my biggest secret, and it wasn't even enough for her. She had to snoop around my meeting, then treat it like a game. She had seen Pa's burned-up hands. This was no game. And now because of her big mouth, not only were we at extra risk, but folks at school treated me like some carnival sideshow freak.

After school she was waiting for me at our normal meeting spot for the walk home. I walked right past her.

"Cub," she called. "Hang on. I shouldn't have blabbed."

I turned and faced her. "Or spied while I was talking with your grandpa."

She nodded and walked up slowly to me. I stayed where I was.

"Yeah, or that. And I'm sorry."

"Fine," I said.

She stared at me for a long moment, then smiled slightly, shaking her head in disbelief.

She said, "You just don't understand what a kick I got out of hearing all that wild stuff. All morning I was waiting to talk to you about it, just suffering because it was so exciting and I knew I couldn't say a word to anyone but you."

Jail. The orphanage. The only family I have getting burned so bad by this evil snake of a man that he almost died.

"'Suffering'?" I said. "You know nothing."

I walked on by myself.

Pa wasn't there when I got home, so I made a halfhearted check on the garden, then dropped into the porch rocker, feeling wore out and unsure of everything. Pa was too hardheaded to know a good plan when he heard one. And Rebecca, the one person I thought I could trust, had ruined things for me at school, and maybe even worse. I sat there, staring up at the gray curls of cloud above, feeling wretched and solitary until I reached a point where my mind just couldn't go on anymore.

"Wake up, boy."

The voice rang out right in my face and I snapped to attention, eyes popping open wide. Pa's face was right there in front of me.

I rubbed my eyes and stared. Was he smiling? That had become almost a foreign practice at our house. Maybe I was still dreaming.

"Where were you, Pa?"

"Went to talk to Yunsen. I wasn't too happy about him talking to you, but he meant well. I saw Rebecca there too."

"Great," I groaned.

I got up from the rocker to go lie down inside.

"Hang on there. I've been thinking about what you said last night."

That woke me up. I sat back down.

"You have? You seemed so mad about it."

He gave me a funny look.

"I seemed mad? Boy, you were the one with your blood boiling. I never seen you that . . . well, not mad exactly. But I've never seen you so danged strong-headed."

You could call it strong-headed, I guessed. But I'd been mad too.

"And that got me to thinking," Pa went on. "I ain't slept a bit, just weighing things up to see if maybe there was some sense in what you'd said. I even went to visit your ma to see what she thought of your idea."

This could be good, I thought.

"And she agreed it's a pretty fool plan, but that it does have some good parts. But then I talked to that horse skinner I know. Cost me two gallons, but I got some good information."

He leaned in, eyes wide, and said, "This Salvatore fellow is working for the North Side Gang. He's under Nicky Merlino himself."

Nicky "No Shadow" Merlino and his crew had made a name for themselves in the papers. They were powerful, violent, and battling the one and only Al Capone, the boss of the bosses, for the liquor trade. How could this possibly be good news?

"Maybe the Feds would get him," Pa said. "He's a big fish. There could even be a reward!"

"That's what I was saying, Pa. They'd arrest him. And we get rid of the shine. Get that farm."

Pa shook his head and raised his palms up to me. "One thing at a time. We focus on Salvatore for now. Then we'll see."

I jumped up out of the rocker and said, "No. Don't you see? The same thing will just happen again. If we keep on living here, we'll never stop shining."

Pa stepped back, staring at me wild-eyed. Neither one of us had expected me to flare up like that.

"I thought you'd be happy about this," he said. "Heck, it was your idea."

To be honest, I couldn't square it either. I should have been glad. But every time I caught sight of the backs of his hands, every time I saw those papery strips of red skin peeling off, I knew inside me that we had to get out of shining forever. And seeing the way he'd come alive out there at that old farm, everything had felt perfect like the old days. It was like he had already forgiven me.

I said, "I just want to put things right. And I can."

He sighed and said, "Look, I can ask about that white house. I'll ask. But you got to tell me one thing first."

"What?"

"When did you get to be so dang stubborn? I've known mules who were more agreeable."

I grinned at him. "Yeah, I wonder who I got it from."

He smiled back at me.

"We can do this, Pa. We can get out of all this. Away from Salvatore. Done with shining for good. But it'll take the both of us."

"The both of us?" he said, the smile falling off his face. "That means you don't go sneaking off behind my back."

"Of course not."

He pressed his lips together for a long moment.

"Maybe we can give it a shot," he said slowly. "I will say that I like the sound of it. Honest living. No more burns. Farming."

Things were far from perfect, but at least we were fighting on the same side again.

CHAPTER
18

OUR PLAN WAS STILL MISSING a key ingredient, and we headed for Mr. Yunsen's to see if he could help us with transport. I hadn't told Pa what people were saying at school and hoped Rebecca wasn't at her house. I could only deal with so many problems at a time.

On the walk, Pa said, "It's dangerous. Salvatore has partners up North. A whole gang of 'em. And I don't think the sheriff will be too happy with all this going on right under his nose. Everybody will take a good look at him too."

"So let 'em. If we're not shining anymore, he can't arrest us."

Pa sighed. "I think the sheriff has his own understanding of the law. And this business with the Feds is going to be tricky. We made fools out of 'em for years," he said with a sad laugh.

We reached the Yunsen home, and Rebecca was nowhere in sight. I sat next to Pa at the big formal table and we told Mr. Yunsen everything: our plan for Salvatore, our new life farming at the white house, and how we needed his help transporting the barrels we had stored in the tree.

Mr. Yunsen heard us out. I explained how I'd done the numbers and that it wasn't some crazy dream. Pa played up the story by twisting his burned hand in front of Mr. Yunsen's face like some horrible claw.

"I wish I could help, Earl," Mr. Yunsen said. "Because I truly admire what you are doing. Not one person has stood up to Salvatore and his organization, and that goes for shiners and police alike. But I retired from the bootlegging business on account of my duty to Rebecca. I cannot risk arrest."

Rebecca. As much as I wanted to be mad at her for this too, I couldn't. She and her grandpa had to look out for themselves.

We offered him money, offered to fix up that giant house, we offered everything we could think of. But as time wore on, we had to give in. There was just no convincing him. My plan was crumbling already.

"We'll just have to sell it some other way," I said. "Maybe local."

Pa said, "It's almost a thousand gallons. And you said it yourself, the good prices are in other towns. We can't walk it there," he said. That wooden sound had come back into his voice.

I knew exactly four people with an automobile—Mr. Salvatore, the sheriff, Mr. Yunsen, and the man who hitched his Ford to that old mare. At the moment, the horse fella looked like our best bet.

Mr. Yunsen shifted in his seat and said, "Once again, gentlemen, I do apologize that I can't be of assistance. It's just, well, you understand, family first."

Pa slumped lower in his seat and said, "Maybe I should just give Salvatore the first batch like he wanted. Then we'd have a while to figure things out."

We had a week and a half before Mr. Salvatore would be

back for the first load. The memory of him making himself all comfortable on our porch made me shiver. I wanted him out of our lives as soon as possible.

I pushed my chair back to leave, and Mr. Yunsen nodded awkwardly to us.

From the opposite side of the room, someone called out, "Wait. Don't go yet."

It was Rebecca. She looked at me as she walked up to her grandpa.

"Please help them," she said.

Mr. Yunsen furrowed his brow. "Were you spying again?"

She looked down at the ground and said, "I was spying because, well, because I'm nosy. And because I knew something bad was going on and I made it worse."

Mr. Yunsen said, "Rebecca, what are you talking about?"

"I made things bad for Cub at school, and I owe it to him to make it up somehow. If you're not going to help them just because of me, then I'll feel doubly worse."

"Rebecca, dear, that is most kind of you, but this has the potential to be dangerous."

"What's dangerous is letting criminals come into town, take over the police, and threaten your friends."

I felt my cheeks warm and I hoped Rebecca didn't notice me blush. She was trying to put things right between us. And this was a heck of a start.

"It's the right thing to do, Grandpa. And it's just driving."

Mr. Yunsen pursed his lips then said to her, "It is true that it would be much safer to keep these criminals away from our town. And it would be two, three trips max. Really no different than my normal trips out of town."

"Please, Grandpa."

"Very well. I will assist in my small way," he said, turning back to Pa and me.

Before we could say a word, Rebecca kissed her grandpa's cheek and dashed back around the corner.

The sky had turned pink and the first stars were already out by the time the three of us spilled out the back door to figure out how much shine the Buick could hold. When Pa first saw that car, he squealed like a little girl.

Mr. Yunsen popped the hood, and while he and I discussed quantities and prices, Pa pored over what he said was a Master Six engine. Mr. Yunsen was already planning to make two trips out of town in the next couple of days and was certain he could sell a full load each trip. He even offered to take Pa to the Federal Department of Justice in Knoxville so he could talk to the agents there. Pa just nodded and ran his fingers over the engine's workings.

We said our farewells, and Mr. Yunsen promised me he'd say goodbye to Rebecca for me. Me and Pa walked down Elm talking nonstop about everything that needed doing. We would have to unload the tree. The final mash would need to be run, then we'd have to take the still apart. With Pa hurt, I'd have to do nearly all the work.

As we walked down the sidewalk, Pa stopped short.

"You go on. I'm going to go talk to somebody. I'll meet you at home."

"Where you going, Pa?"

"I told you I'd see about that white house."

CHAPTER 19

PA HADN'T BEEN ABLE TO track down the man who knew about the white house, but he did get an advance on a few gallons of shine and came back with food. With his hurt arms he could hardly help bring the shine out of the tree, but he insisted he could carry something. I wedged a small jug under his armpit, and he did a goosestep shuffle toward the house. The glass slipped out and shattered on a hunk of limestone. We couldn't afford to lose even an ounce of shine now.

Pa sulked off to tend the fire while I scrambled in and out of the tree, scratching myself going both ways in the dark. I made a pyramid of barrels inside the coop, hoping the chickens wouldn't get curious and peck into them. I was too busy to deal with a bunch of drunken hens.

The October night was silent as I crunched through the dead pine needles with the last jug of moonshine we'd ever make. Pa was right behind me, his white bandages glowing in the moonlight.

I had only about four hours before I'd have to load the Buick, then go in for a full day of school, where I'd be bombarded with questions about some imaginary Mafia life I wanted nothing to do with. And if word reached Pounder or the teachers, things could get even worse for us. Just thinking about it made me tired, but I knew I was too worked up to sleep.

We walked in the back door and Pa went straight for his room. When I picked up the kerosene lamp on the table, he asked, "You're not tired?"

"No. I'm going to sit here a while."

I lit the lamp and our little kitchen glowed yellow and warm all around me.

"And do what?" he asked from the doorway.

"Nothing."

He paused for a second and scratched the back of his neck. "Mind if I join you?"

I shrugged. Pa walked back into the kitchen and said, "Because I know something we can do that's better than nothing."

"What?"

"Have a late-night feast."

Pa pulled the frying pan off the wall, and using only the very tips of his fingers to work, started frying some catfish he'd picked up in town. I cut up some okra. Pa had brought biscuits too. They were hard from the cold air, but still good.

We got busy preparing it all, moving around each other and working smoothly like we always had at the still. I put the okra on our wooden plates and Pa dumped big steaming chunks of fish on top and splashed some vinegar over it. We sat down at three in the morning, and just as I was about to take my first bite, I noticed Pa staring at me.

"What?" I asked.

135

"You know, you are just the spitting image of your ma."

"Great, Pa. I always wanted to look like a girl."

Folks before had told me what she had looked like—tall for a woman, pretty hair, big ears, but I could never put those pieces together in my head for a real image of her.

"Not how you look. I mean the way you are."

"That ain't possible."

"You know, it's funny. Ya'll have got the same way of lighting a fire, using huge pieces of kindling when anybody with common sense would start with pieces half the size."

I smiled and forked a chunk of fried catfish into my mouth.

"And the same way of treating a cut or a burn, putting on a medicine fast and hard, not worrying if a fella's in pain, just making sure the treatment's on there good."

"Maybe you just got the same way of being a baby."

"Well, that too. But mostly it's that the both of you ain't got any quit in you. There were a lot of times when she was sick, whole months, when a regular person would've flat gave up. She was scared and she was hurting, but she kept fighting 'til the last second. And you're the same way. I just didn't see it 'til now."

I was plumb embarrassed by that point, but he wouldn't stop. "Think about how strong you've been through all this. School for the first time, police trouble, a gangster on our tails . . . And did you get scared?"

I looked at him for a long moment.

"Yes. Every second."

"But you fought through it," he said, pointing at me. "And we haven't quit yet. That's in our blood. And that's something that'll never die."

136

CHAPTER 20

MR. YUNSEN ARRIVED WITH THE rising sun on Friday, dressed in a black suit that matched his hearse perfectly. It was up to me to load nearly three hundred gallons of shine into the Buick. I packed the shine everywhere I could, including inside the empty casket in the back. Two little pint jars went where the head would go, and then I made a full body with some bigger barrels. It was a perfect fit.

Pa crouched down next to the hearse's shiny spoked wheel and asked Mr. Yunsen, "What are you going to do if somebody stops you?"

"If I've got a full load of liquor, I'd have to make a quick escape."

"You think you could outrun 'em?"

"I'd love to find out," Mr. Yunsen said with a sly smile.

With my back feeling broken from having hefted all the barrels, I closed the little white curtains hanging on each of the rear windows and told Mr. Yunsen good luck. Pa and I watched him drive away with nearly half of everything we owned.

I had to run to get to school on time, which was a cruel kind of torture because I was dreading class. Right as the last group of people was heading in the door, Rebecca rushed up and grabbed my arm.

"Hey, I fixed it."

"Yeah, thanks for getting your grandpa—"

"No, I mean here," she said, then rushed inside without another word.

I followed her in and was instantly mobbed by half the class.

Russ asked, "Cub, are you really Al Capone's nephew? Rebecca swore it."

Oh no. What had she told people now?

Frankie said, "And she said you're scheming to rob Fort Knox. Is that true? Because it sounded like malarkey to me."

He stood there cross-armed, frowning at me, and the genius of Rebecca's new rumors dawned on me.

I smiled and said, "Oh yeah. Me and Uncle Al are going to dynamite it. I'm building a mansion out of gold bars."

Frankie turned and threw his hands up to the class. "I *told* you it weren't true!"

Shane stepped up and said, "But his pa really is a crook."

Rebecca pushed her way into the group.

"And I'm the queen of England. You'll believe anything."

Miss Pounder came in and everyone dashed for their seats.

I leaned up to Rebecca's desk and said, "You actually did fix it. Thank you."

"Wasn't hard. I told you everybody here is dumber than donkey teeth."

By lunch the class debate had turned to whether Roscoe had flunked fourth grade four or five times, and no one even gave me a second look when I joined the kickball game.

We had penmanship class after lunch, and halfway through I realized I really had to go. I balanced my dip pen on the inkwell as best I could and got up from my desk.

Miss Pounder sat upright in her big special chair and cleared her throat all loud at me like her pipes were clogged with porridge.

"Cub, where do you think you're going?"

"I'll be back. Don't you worry," I said, not slowing.

She jumped out of that throne of hers and cut me off before I could reach the door. She stood there squared off on me like she was Dempsey in the ring.

"You can't just leave, Cub. Not without telling me where you're going."

They had a lot of rules at that school. A lot. And I abided by them as best I could. But there was one rule that was so bizarre that I refused to honor it.

In my most polite voice, I said, "Miss Pounder, I will be back. That's all I have to say."

She folded her arms across her chest and smirked at me.

"If you need to visit the outhouse, Cub, all you have to do is ask."

"I will do no such thing."

Her big head jerked back, and she let out a little yelp at my defiance.

I said, "It seems disgusting that you want people to tell you their business like that. Even a dog doesn't have to ask permission."

The class was in hysterics. A couple of the boys were even applauding. I sidestepped her, ready to bob and weave under a left hook, but she was glued to the floor, silent. Two and a half minutes later, I was back in my desk practicing my penmanship.

Nobody talked about it after that. Not Pounder, not anybody in my class. But my little protest apparently struck a chord with the others. That afternoon, two other students came and went during Pounder's class like civilized people.

· · ·

After school, I walked Rebecca to her turnoff, then continued on to the house. Pa was sitting at the table, surrounded by crumpled dollar bills and Eight O'Clock Coffee cans full of coins.

"That house is for sale. The owner has been trying to get rid of it for two years. But it's eleven hundred dollars up front."

My legs were shaking with joy. "And we got enough money?" I asked.

Pa looked up and smiled kind of embarrassed-like, trying to grip a pencil between the fingers of his bad hand. He had been marking on a ledger in big, ugly swoops. "That's what I'm trying to figure out. Yunsen came by with over nine hundred dollars. Tomorrow he's selling another three hundred gallons. But I'm still working the numbers here to see what we need for the rest."

"Can I give it a shot, Pa?"

Pa pushed the ledger over to me. He wiped his forehead with his sleeve and sighed. "I feel like I been in a fight."

A sheet and a half of paper later, I looked over at him and grimaced. "It's not impossible, Pa."

"No?"

"If we get seven fifty a gallon for the rest, plus maybe two hundred dollars for the still, it would work out."

"Did you say seven fifty a gallon?" he asked, gripping my arm. Salvatore was paying him two and a quarter.

"It's not impossible."

A powerful thunderstorm came that evening. Pa and I spent the rest of the weekend indoors, pacing the floors and talking about what we'd be doing if it weren't raining. On Sunday morning, the ground was nothing but puddles. The garden had flooded, and little rivers ran down the rows. I sat out under the leaky porch roof, waiting for the rain to slack off to a drizzle so I could clean the still.

By late afternoon the lightning storm had passed, and I told Pa I'd clean the still and get it ready myself.

He said, "I can help. My left hand is almost working now."

"You shouldn't get your bandages wet. It won't take me more than an hour."

"Then I'll go see Yunsen and set things up for tomorrow morning."

I wished I'd thought to go to Rebecca's house. We went in, and following a quick chicken dinner, I set off into the woods with a jug of vinegar and salt I'd mixed up to clean the copper. On the trail I heard the sorrowful *hoo-ah-hoo* of a mourning dove somewhere up in the big tree, but couldn't place him. Staring at the tree, I realized it did not look as commanding it usually did, maybe because I knew its trunk was now nearly empty after two days of sales.

It was sundown when I got there, and the clearing was a soupy mess. There were some logs and kindling in our stack under the sweetgum tree, but even those had been hit hard by rain. After nearly half an hour I had a sputtering little fire going next to the pot. I set some more logs around it to dry them and got to work cleaning the copper with an old wire brush.

My eyes were stinging in the wet wood's smoke, and after a few minutes of scrubbing, my hands were cold and raw. I could kind of see my reflection in the still, so I knew it was somewhat cleaner, but in the dark it was hard to tell how much. I dumped the rest of the vinegar over the top, then headed down to the creek to fetch more rinsing water. The water off the wet leaves ran up the cuffs of my overalls and froze my legs. Somewhere back toward the house, a twig snapped, and I stopped mid-step.

Standing there as quiet as I could, I heard another snap. Too loud for a squirrel or rabbit, I thought, but maybe a big buck. I waited a full sixty heartbeats, but only heard the creek gurgling and water dripping down off the pine needles. I filled my jugs with water and walked silently across the dead leaves like Pa had taught me. I got back to the clearing to find Mr. Salvatore standing next to the fire.

I gasped and dropped the jugs of water. Mr. Salvatore stood between the fire and the still, hat pulled down over his eyes and mud almost up to the knees of his suit pants. He looked right at me, no expression on his face, hands shoved into his pockets.

"Why is everything taken apart?" he asked.

I scrambled to pick up the jugs and walked over to the parts of the still, watching Mr. Salvatore out of the corner of my eye. I felt a slow raking over my insides.

Mr. Salvatore took a step toward me and yelled, "Why is everything taken apart?"

His voice came out harsh, like his vocal cords were packed with crushed glass.

"Um, I had to clean it."

Mr. Salvatore watched as I poured the creek water down the side of the kettle, splashing it all over my legs. I busied myself rinsing the pot, but I could feel Mr. Salvatore's eyes on me.

"How'd you know where the still was?" I asked.

"The sheriff told me. Plus, I've been here before," he added with a menacing grin.

I looked down and kept scrubbing the pot.

"Where's your father?"

Pa wasn't at home, I realized. In the reflection off the gleaming copper, I looked myself straight in the eye and thought, I can get us out of this. Salvatore thinks I'm just some dumb backwoods kid. I took a deep breath, turned and faced him, ready to say Pa was at a neighbor's, at church, anywhere. Other words came out.

"He's at the doctor 'cause you burned him."

The expression on Salvatore's face didn't change, and we stared at each other for a long moment.

"That was nothing," he said, taking a step toward me. "What we call a 'warning shot.'"

He walked up until he was within arm's distance, then took off his hat and wiped his brow with his coat sleeve.

"Kid, that was a trip to the ice cream parlor compared to the things you see growing up in a family like mine."

A crime family, I thought. Mafia.

Mr. Salvatore went on, "You and me aren't all that different, kid. Brought up in the family business, outside the law. You know as well as I do there ain't no going against it."

His family was nothing like mine. I was nothing like him. And as a matter of fact, I had gone against the family business.

He looked off into the woods, then straightened his suit coat and put his hat back on. "Plans have changed. First delivery Tuesday night."

Tuesday? That was in two days.

"You said we had ten days," I said.

"Are you dense, kid? I just said the plans had changed. A hundred gallons."

Nothing was ready. Pa hadn't talked to the Feds yet. And worst of all, we no longer had a hundred gallons in the tree to give him.

"But a hundred gallons is too much."

"I know you've got hundreds, kid, your pa told me himself. And you've already had your warning."

It was impossible. He did not understand that.

"We need more time," I said.

"Tuesday," he said, and I could tell his patience was fraying.

"What if we're not ready?"

With his hands on his knees, he leaned down so we were eye to eye. He spoke in a soft, simple voice.

"Then one of you will be burying the other in this mud hole you call home," he said. "Now we're gonna go wait for your pop to get back."

Every muscle in my body was burning to tear into him, to grab the shovel and knock his head clean off. He rocked back on his heels and hitched up his pants, and I knew he could crush me like a pill bug. I had to think. Pa could be back at any moment. I needed to warn him somehow before he got back to the house.

I said, "But if I don't get this mash going tonight we won't have your shine by Tuesday."

Mr. Salvatore didn't say anything, and I scrambled to start a fire under the big pot, blackening up all that metal I'd just cleaned. When the flame had caught well, I turned and said, "If you want to help, I'd sure appreciate it. Shouldn't take us more than an hour and a half or so."

Mr. Salvatore grimaced. "I got things to do," he said. "Two days, I'll be back."

I didn't look up from the fire, just listened as Salvatore crunched his way back toward the house. I prayed Pa was still gone and that I could find him before Mr. Salvatore did. I poured the rest of the water over the fire, and as it sizzled itself out, I took off running.

CHAPTER

21

AN OLD GAME TRAIL RAN from the clearing to the back side of town, but I didn't have the daylight or the time to find it. I ran what I thought was the straightest course south, jumping over logs as sycamore branches whipped me in the face. With one hand out in front of me and the other to the side for balance, I slipped and slid my way through the mud. Going down a hill, my boots lost their grip, and I fell face-first into a pine, crunching my shoulder into the trunk. My hand went into some rocks, and I felt the skin on my palm flap open. I jumped up and kept running.

My boots and legs were caked with mud, dragging me down. I kept thumping on across Main Street without seeing a soul. As I started down Rebecca's turnoff, a voice called out next to me.

"Cub?"

I recognized the voice, but my feet wouldn't stop in time. I half turned and said, "Pa?" right as my legs flew out from under me and I skidded across the wet dirt road.

Pa ran over and lifted me up, but as soon as I was upright, a cramp from running so hard doubled me back over. With the cuff of his coat, Pa tried to wipe the grime off my face.

"Mr. Salvatore," I said. "Did you see him?"

"Salvatore? No."

I exhaled hard and forced myself to stand straight. It was dark and there was little moonlight, but Pa led me off the road regardless. We didn't need to be seen.

"You saw Salvatore?" he asked.

I nodded. He pulled me close with his good arm and asked, "What did he do?"

"I'm fine, Pa. It was just words."

He waited.

"But he said if we weren't ready he was gonna kill us."

Pa's eyes flashed fire and he said, "I'm going to kill him myself, you watch me."

"He's coming back in two days."

"Two days?" Pa grabbed me with trembling hands and started leading me toward Rebecca's.

Pa pounded on the front door, and Mr. Yunsen jumped when he got a look at me. When I saw my face in the bathroom mirror, I understood why—I was all dirt, blood, and mud.

Pa led me to their old claw-foot bathtub and I stripped off my heavy flannel and overalls and got in wearing just my underwear. I was mighty glad they had running water here until I felt how cold it was. I shivered and shook as twigs and mud seeped out of my hair and into the tub.

When I could finally talk, I told Pa what had happened with the still.

"You did good, boy, tricking Mr. Salvatore. I can't say that I would have been so clever."

Mr. Yunsen came in with a towel, and Pa told him the story.

"Rebecca," Mr. Yunsen called through the open door.

"No!" I yelled.

"She's not coming in. Don't worry."

When the water finally started to run clear off my head, I had another look at my face in the mirror. I was scratched from branches in every way possible, and it looked like I'd been beat with a broom. There were drops of blood on the white tile floor. My blood. I held my right hand out and it was slit right across the palm. I clenched my hand tight so I didn't have to look at it.

Pa turned to Mr. Yunsen. "Look at this cut here."

He forced open my fingers, and I watched my hand pool up with dark blood.

"Have you got any iodine?" Pa asked.

"I'm afraid I'll have to fetch my needle and catgut as well," Mr. Yunsen said and left the room.

I spun toward Pa, nearly slipping on the wet floor. I asked, "What's the needle for?"

Pa smiled and held up his bandaged arm and said, "The two of us are just a mess."

I put on the clothes Mr. Yunsen had brought for me. He said he was sorry he didn't have anything my size, but if it was between wearing his clothes and wearing Rebecca's, I'd take his funeral clothes every time. Dressed in long black slacks and a dress shirt that was about five sizes too big, I walked out of the tub room and found Rebecca waiting for me with a lamp.

"A little grandpa!" she said.

I felt my ears burn, but I smiled as best I could and shuffled into the main room. Rebecca had made a fire and set a large plush chair in front of the wood-burning stove. Still shaking slightly, I sank into the chair. Rebecca began toweling my hair as I warmed my sore face.

147

Pa and Mr. Yunsen returned, Pa holding a gold kerosene lamp and Mr. Yunsen clutching his dark leather bag. He reached in for his instruments.

All his tools for dead folks were in there, and I wondered if I might faint before we even got started.

Rebecca went to fetch more lamps. Pa leaned in and whispered, "Now you get to show her how brave you are."

I didn't say anything, just watched Mr. Yunsen set items on the little metal tray. One brown bottle that read IODINE. One small ivory semicircle, like a fishhook. One roll of thin cord. And in Mr. Yunsen's bony fingers was a pair of metal tweezers.

Rebecca walked behind my chair and patted the top of my head. I jumped a little and was happy she couldn't see my face. Every heartbeat brought a fresh pulse of pain just as sure as Mr. Salvatore was there stabbing my palm with a jackknife. The worst of it, however, was yet to come.

Under the light of the fire and five lamps, Mr. Yunsen stripped off a hair-thin piece of fiber and threaded it through a tiny eye in the ivory hook, which he held pinched in the tweezers. He began to tell a story, speaking in a slow, almost hypnotizing voice.

"I once met a man who had traveled the world many times over. He told me of a most interesting practice they use in India."

Mr. Yunsen dabbed the dark blood from my palm with a towel and repositioned the kerosene lamp. I could feel sweat forming on my temples. Just do it already, I thought.

"To treat an open wound such as this, local medicine men would harvest a large species of ant, an insect roughly the size of our hummingbirds."

Mr. Yunsen balanced the pointy end of the white hook over my palm and kept talking in a low, soothing rhythm.

"This was a fierce creature. And throughout India it was known for its powerful jaws, which would lock down like the bite of a snapping turtle."

I felt the skin tighten as the curled hook pressed hard against the flesh of my palm, then sunk in. It was like he was shoving broken glass inside and I had to fight to steady my hand. Before I could look away, the hook and thread popped back out on the other side of the cut, bursting through the skin from the inside. Rebecca gasped as little spurts of blood pumped out of me and mixed with the sweat. Mr. Yunsen kept talking like nothing had happened.

"They would hold this colossal ant above the injury and it would bite down, clamping the wound shut. With a sharp twist they'd snatch the ant's torso off, leaving the head to hang there for days, sealing the wound with its jaws."

At this point I heard Pa lean in and say all excited, "Please tell me you have these ants, Herbert."

"No, I'm afraid I only have this catgut and whalebone."

Black spots before me made it impossible to watch, but I felt the point of the hook dip into my skin again, turn, then explode back through the skin. I was close to passing out and I peeked over just in time to see a tiny knot slide down the cord and rest on my palm.

Mr. Yunsen dabbed at my hand with his towel. "Congratulations, Cub, you are the second living patient on whom I've performed this procedure."

I sank back and gave Rebecca a weak smile. Sweat was still dripping off my face onto my fancy shirt, but I had survived.

When I had steadied myself, I said, "Thank you, Mr. Yunsen. Who was the first?"

"Myself," he said with a smile. "Now, let's discuss what we're going to do about this Salvatore."

CHAPTER 22

PA PULLED OVER TWO MORE chairs and the four of us sat there in the flickering firelight asking each other questions none of us knew the answers to.

Mr. Yunsen asked, "Could Mr. Salvatore be waiting at your house?"

"What if he comes to check again tomorrow?" Rebecca added.

I didn't figure Mr. Salvatore would wait us out there at the house, but maybe my acting hadn't fooled him as well as I'd thought. Staring at that little black knot sewn into my hand made me wonder if my whole plan was going to unravel before it got started.

"Two days," Pa muttered.

I could hear the seconds ticking away in my head.

Mr. Yunsen said, "Gentlemen, I have the final sale arranged, but not until next week. Not to mention the fact that you have not spoken with the federal agents in Knoxville."

"What if you talked to them tomorrow?" I asked.

"We could, I suppose. It would leave the agents little time to prepare, but we don't have much choice."

"Could we sell the rest of the shine there too?" Pa asked.

Hearing him ask that made me feel glad even in my weakened state. He hadn't given up on me or my plan yet.

Mr. Yunsen hesitated, then said, "I do know a man there. It would not be a typical sale, but it could work."

Rebecca jumped to her feet looking all excited and turned to Pa.

"Make sure to tell the Feds that Mr. Salvatore is a big-time gangster. That he's in it with Nicky Merlino. That it's a matter of national security. Then they'll put their best men on the case."

Pa nodded awkwardly, and Mr. Yunsen stepped in.

"I'm sure Salvatore is just a petty criminal," Mr. Yunsen said. "And the Feds will do their job, there's no need to worry about that."

I could see plain in his face that Mr. Yunsen was trying to keep me and Pa from overworrying. Rebecca was going in a different direction though.

"Of course, if he is a gangster," she said, staring into the fire as she thought it all out, "that means he's in a gang. And the rest of the gang probably wouldn't like it if you got one of them locked up."

"Now, Rebecca," Mr. Yunsen said, "let's not get carried away."

Mr. Salvatore certainly acted like some kind of big-shot crook. He had a big car, probably had lots of guns. He looked like the men in the papers, either the mug shots where they were holding up numbers or the crime scene pictures where everybody was laid out in the street with their suits full of bullet holes.

Pa turned to me and said, "We're going to have to keep watch for Salvatore all night."

It was true. I wondered if Pa would let me sleep with the shotgun.

Mr. Yunsen said, "Rebecca and I would be delighted if you would be our guests for the evening."

Staying in this giant house sounded a whole lot safer than sleeping in our little shack. And me and Rebecca could stay up late and talk and plan.

"Can we, Pa?" I asked.

Pa turned to Mr. Yunsen and asked, "You sure? We don't want to be a bother."

"It would be our pleasure. We'll have supper and you can sleep in our spare room. Tomorrow we'll pick up the shine and drive up to Knoxville."

"We'll take you up on it then. Thank you very much," Pa said, then turned to Rebecca. "Both of you."

I thought I'd give it a shot and see if I could ride along, even though I had school. "And can I go to Knoxville too?"

To my surprise, Pa said, "I was thinking the same thing."

"And me too?" Rebecca asked.

Mr. Yunsen shook his head. "I'm afraid not. But you can help me prepare supper."

She groaned, but was still smiling.

"Say hi to Miss Pounder for me tomorrow," I told her.

"Don't forget your note this time, dum-dum," she said, then got up and went to the kitchen.

As she and her grandpa made supper, me and Pa huddled close to the fire and talked about what to say to the government men. Pa told me flat out that he was nervous.

"Big towns are different. And those big-time agents might take a notion to ask me how I happen to know so much about moonshining."

I tried to settle him as best I could and said, "Just tell 'em that Mr. Salvatore will be at the house tomorrow night and that he'll have loads of liquor. And that they should put him in jail."

"They might want to put me in jail too. We've been shining for over ten years."

Pa made a fair point. But by the time he went in there to talk to the law, we'd have sold all the liquor and the still. We'd be out of the business. Of course, they could probably charge us with all sorts of stuff if they knew the details, but we were going straight now. We were getting on the right side of the law. A fella's got to have a chance to do that, right?

He went on, "I'm hoping I can work something out with 'em. They just got to understand how hard times were when I started. A man and a baby can't share a potato for their supper."

Rebecca called us from the far side of the room and I walked over to that big long table and saw that it was heaped with every kind of food in the world—pork and gravy, macaroni, collards, pumpkin, corn bread, and some other things I wasn't familiar with.

It was the fanciest meal I'd ever eaten, and I was glad I had on Mr. Yunsen's church clothes for it, no matter how big they were on me. Mr. Yunsen had me howling, telling stories about running liquor with Pa back in the old days, and when I'd finally calmed myself from laughing, I prayed the Feds hadn't heard those same stories.

After supper Rebecca showed me all around her big, empty house and showed me her room as well. Fine pillows and flowery smells were what I imagined, walking upstairs, but there was none of that. There was none of anything, in fact, save for a plain bed and a sewing machine built into a table. Rebecca led me to the machine and then fished out a bright red spool of thread from a basket beneath.

"This one's from Chicago," she said, holding up the ruby-colored thread.

"Wow, you use it much?"

"Not yet. I'm scared to start because once I do it'll run out real fast. My folks sent it to me."

We sat on the bed, and I kept looking at the sewing machine. There wasn't anything else in the room, so I wasn't sure what else to look at.

I held up a dangling sleeve and asked her, "You think you could fix this?"

"You mean shorten your clothes? Or sew on your hand some more?"

"The clothes, dum-dum."

She got a real proud look on her face and said, "If I had time I could make it perfect. My ma showed me how, and we used to make clothes for everybody, some even to sell."

"You always got nice clothes," I told her. "And a nice house too."

She smiled and asked, "How come you never invited me to your house?"

"Ain't much to see," I said.

We sat quiet on the edge of the bed, Rebecca swinging her legs in front of her, me sitting up straight, with my hands sweating on the thighs of her grandpa's dress pants. I wondered if I was supposed to do or say something then. We sat silently and the room started feeling real warm and I realized I'd forgotten to breathe.

Pa's voice rang out behind us, and I jumped, bouncing up off her bed and nearly crashing into the sewing machine.

"Hey, boy, it's almost midnight."

I mumbled good night to Rebecca and walked into the hall with Pa. We were sharing a room with two beds, a normal bed and a giant one with four wooden posts. Strung over the top, there was a big white canopy that floated over the mattress like a ship's sail.

Pa approached the bigger bed slowly and ran his fingers over the carved wooden posts.

"You want this one?" he asked.

I laughed and shook my head. "I'll take the little one."

"Dang," he said. "If this bed roof falls in the night, come help me."

I was glad me and Pa weren't in our shack, noses pressed to the window, praying we didn't see headlights. It struck me kind of funny how I felt more relaxed in this old haunted house, sleeping under the same roof as the old man I had pegged as a killer and the girl who'd thought I was slow. As I drifted off to sleep, I decided that I would invite Rebecca to my new house.

CHAPTER

23

BEFORE I'D EVEN CRACKED MY EYES open that next morning, my head was racing with thoughts of everything that had to go right for us that day. It was like we were playing poker and if we drew just one bad hand we'd lose everything.

Not only did we have to get all that liquor into town, somebody had to buy it. Not to mention the fact that Pa was putting his faith in the same folks we'd been dodging since I was born. There was a lot at stake—everything really. Today we'd see just what kind of odds we were up against.

The tent ceiling over Pa's bed had not crashed on him in the night, which I took as a good sign for the day. It wasn't even light out yet, but Pa was gone. He'd left me some clothes folded on top of a chest of drawers. Nobody even lived in this room and they still had a full set of drawers, not half for each like me and Pa back home.

After a quick breakfast of toast and muscadine jelly, I said goodbye to Rebecca and we piled into the hearse. Mr. Yunsen, Pa, and I sat in a row on the front bench seat, while an empty coffin that would be the final resting place for our last batch of shine lay in the back. The day was promising adventure, and my insides were starting to tingle until we got closer to our house and I spotted the deep tire ruts Mr. Salvatore's car had cut into the road.

"Is he still there?" I asked Pa.

Mr. Yunsen edged the front of the hearse past the corn until we could just spy the house. I leaned up so close my breath fogged the windshield, straining to see any sign of Mr. Salvatore or his car.

"He's gone," Mr. Yunsen said finally and swung the car in and around, backing it right up to the coop. It was a short haul for the last load of shine, but with only one working pair of hands between us, me and Pa had a hard time fitting those barrels into the coffin. Mr. Yunsen tried to help, but on his first barrel, his spine cracked like a machine gun and he limped away. By seven o'clock we had loaded the hearse. Except for the giant copper still sitting in our woods, me and Pa could have passed for regular old dirt farmers.

We settled in for the long ride, Mr. Yunsen driving fast and me taking in every sight I could out the window. We passed little towns that looked almost identical to Hidden Orchard, save for a few odd details that made them seem strange and mysterious.

"Pa, this place has got sidewalks on both sides of the street."

"Seems wasteful," he said.

We headed down from the hills, the humid air getting thicker in my lungs with every passing mile. Pa said little, staring straight ahead and moving his lips as he practiced what he was going to say.

In the eyes of the law, Pa was a criminal. And he was going to walk into a building full of government men and ask them to help him. What if they didn't believe him? What if they just didn't care? Or what if they cared so much they threw him in jail too?

"Pa, don't tell the agents nothing too bad about what we did, okay?"

He nodded. "I'll make this work. Somehow or other I'll make it work."

Just as I was putting my hopes in our new life and a fresh beginning, I heard a clanging behind the hearse. I spun around to see a police car right on our tail.

"Is it Sheriff Bardo?" Mr. Yunsen asked.

The policeman dropped back, only to speed up again, almost nicking the back of the Buick.

"No. I've never seen him before," I said.

Between flashes of red light, I could make out an angry man in uniform, pointing to the side of the road and mouthing some word over and over. He kept sounding an emergency bell mounted on his car.

"I think he wants us to stop," I said.

"Just like that time outside Memphis, huh, Herbert?" Pa said.

"I could run circles around his little Ford," Mr. Yunsen said, with a hint of challenge in his voice.

I saw that Mr. Yunsen's hand was twitching a little on top of the round gearshift, like he was just dying to get us into high gear. Running from the cops in a car full of shine seemed like a good way to get sent to prison for life. Hopefully Mr. Yunsen didn't have some plan to go out guns blazing.

Pa asked him, "You thinking about getting out of here?" His voice came out fast and nervous.

"You tell me."

I turned toward Pa and asked, "If we ran, could we still go to Knoxville?"

Mr. Yunsen answered for him. "Oh, no. We'd have to lay low for a bit. He'd radio all the big towns."

"But we've got to go to Knoxville today," I said. "We can't give up now."

"Earl?" Mr. Yunsen asked.

Pa was silent, staring pale-faced out the windshield.

"We could say we're on our way to a funeral," Mr. Yunsen offered.

"Please, Pa. We've got to try something."

"Okay," Pa said.

Mr. Yunsen slowed the hearse, parked us right on the side of the road, and rolled down his window. I heard the police cruiser's door slam behind us. A few seconds later a rough, red face appeared, the officer sticking his head so far inside the hearse that if Mr. Yunsen were to raise the window, it would have caught the policeman at the neck.

He studied each of us, and the way his eyes went over us reminded me of the time me and Pa watched a mountain lion scout a herd of deer up in the hills, picking out the easiest prey to kill. The officer's cold gaze finally settled on me. For what felt like a full minute, I looked up at him and gave him a pained half smile.

"How about ya'll tell me what you're doing here?"

"Oh, work I'm afraid," said Mr. Yunsen. "Passing through on our way to a funeral in Knoxville."

"You're working?"

Mr. Yunsen nodded.

"You wouldn't happen to work as a bootlegger, would you?" the officer asked.

"I beg your pardon?" Mr. Yunsen said.

I heard Pa gulp like he was swallowing a spoonful of gravel.

"We got reports of bootleggers coming through here.

Rumrunners coming through in big vehicles. But you wouldn't know anything about that now, would you?"

The officer leaned farther inside the hearse, the rim of his hat scraping the roof. He stared at me.

"How come you ain't in school, boy? Harvest break ain't for weeks."

His cocky tone reminded me of the first time Sheriff Bardo had come to our house. He had laughed at me when I'd gone mute and tucked myself behind Pa's leg. I had nowhere to hide myself now, not unless I wanted to crawl into the back and get in the casket.

Not a foot away from my face, the officer said, "Answer me, boy."

"I finished school. I did it all."

They had told me that finishing school actually took years. I had survived thirty-four days and failed nearly every test.

The policeman asked, "You graduated? How old are you?"

"Sixteen."

"So you're working then?"

"Always."

The officer turned his attention back to Mr. Yunsen and asked, "Do you have any illegal liquor inside this vehicle?"

"Of course not."

"Step out of the vehicle and walk around back. All of you."

I squeezed tight on Pa's leg in case Mr. Yunsen decided to zoom us out of there. Instead, the door clicked open and I saw Mr. Yunsen's black coattails disappear out the driver's door. Me and Pa got out on our side, and the three of us lined up behind the hearse in our suits.

The policeman was huge. He was taller than even Pa and about as wide as all three of us put together. He motioned to the back doors of the hearse, and Mr. Yunsen opened them, exposing the purple velvet interior and the cherrywood coffin. The officer stuck his head in to inspect it, then pulled his head back out to inspect us.

160

"You're going to a funeral, huh?"

I nodded, and the policeman bent down and got right in my face again.

"Okay, Mister Sixteen-Year-Old," he said, "who's the funeral for, then?"

"Miss Eugenia Rawls. Age sixty-eight. Fell off a horse and broke her neck," I said, making it up on the spot.

The policeman raised an eyebrow. I thought for a second I heard Mr. Yunsen chuckle.

"So when we open this casket we'll see her in there?"

My story was all for nothing. He was going to find the shine. Before anybody could move though, Pa broke his silence and spoke.

"Ooh, she's in there all right, but just barely. That was the second biggest woman I ever saw. Took all three of us to get her in there. You should've seen old Wilfred here," Pa said, pointing his thumb at me, "just jumping on top of that casket to fit her in there. Parts kept squirting out. I didn't think we'd ever cram her in there."

The officer's head jerked back about a foot and a half, and I saw his bottom lip quiver.

I tried to keep the rhythm going. "We can open her up if you want, but with this sun . . ." I paused and made a big show of studying the sun's exact position. "I'd imagine the gases will have taken effect. You'd have to help us get her back in there."

"And she could blow," Pa added.

"She very well could," I said.

The officer looked like he'd found a mouse tail in his stew.

With both palms raised, he asked, "So no shine?"

"A body, but no spirits," Mr. Yunsen said.

"All right, let's get you fellas out of here. Follow me and I'll lead you through Coalville."

The cruiser pulled out in front of us, and Mr. Yunsen fell in line right behind it with the hearse.

"The two of you should be in motion pictures," Mr. Yunsen said as we followed our special police escort through town.

We were overcome with a laughing fit, and every time we were able to control ourselves, I'd do an imitation of Pa's voice and say, "And she could blow," and we'd all crack up again. At the end of town, the officer pointed us around him, and I waved him goodbye, and we sped off toward Knoxville for what I prayed was our final illegal sale.

CHAPTER 24

AS WE ROLLED DOWN OUT of the hills and into the flatlands, I took to reading the giant, hand-carved signs posted at the entrance to every little town.

Welcome to Mapleton
The Sunniest Town in Tennessee

Thirty feet farther down the road there would always be an even bigger sign, newer and thrown together with railroad ties and scrap wood.

NO JOBS
TRANSIENTS KEEP MOVING

There were great crowds of people in the streets, some standing in lines, other folks sprawled out in a park, sleeping in the middle of the day. Pa nodded toward one white-haired woman wrapped up in a copy of the *Tennessean* daily and said to me, "That there's a Hoover blanket."

"How come there are so many people around?"

"No job to go to," Pa said. "Maybe just looking for food."

As we neared the Knoxville train depot, the buildings changed from wood and brick to soggy cardboard and riveted sheet metal. There were jumbles of shacks along the road, everything shoved together with pallets, cardboard, and jagged scrap metal. Fires blazed out of dirty trash barrels. Folks stared at us as we rolled by in our big black hearse.

One group of kids a little younger than me started running alongside us. The soles of their shoes were flapping and they were hollering, trying to get a look inside. They probably lived in that big mountain of pallets we just drove by. Makes me and Pa's shack seem like a mansion, I thought. Pa passed 'em each a nickel at the stop sign and I felt a little embarrassed when they looked me over in the church clothes Mr. Yunsen had lent me.

"We must be the only folks in America quitting their jobs," I said.

Pa nodded. "You see how skinny everybody is?"

Walking right through the street was a teenage girl the color of the sidewalk, all knees, elbows, and cheekbones.

"They don't have room to farm here. We can raise chickens, grow potatoes, corn, spinach," Pa said.

"So what do they eat, then?" I asked.

Mr. Yunsen pointed at a long row of people lined up against a brick wall.

"Those people there are waiting for soup. They can get free soup, bread, perhaps a coffee."

And here we were, I thought, trying desperately to wash our hands of the one thing guaranteed to put food on the table. Except we were no longer shining just to get by. Salvatore owned us. I glanced over at the scorched pink skin peeking out from the cuff of Pa's shirt, and that helped shore up my faith that we were doing the right thing.

I read a big sign that said DEPARTMENT OF JUSTICE, KNOXVILLE, and Mr. Yunsen parked next to a long line of black government cars. He shut off the motor, and the three of us sat there, silent.

"You want me to go with you, Pa?"

"No, boy. This is something I've got to take care of myself."

Mr. Yunsen leaned across and said, "No matter what they say to you, Earl, make sure they know that a major bootlegger is going to be in Hidden Orchard tomorrow. If they catch the big shot, they'll be more lenient with you about any past wrongdoings."

Pa looked up at the big, penitentiary-style federal building and shook his head. "I always figured if I came here it'd be in bracelets."

He looked at me for a long moment, and I had the dreadful thought that he was trying to memorize my face in case he didn't come back out. Like he was sacrificing himself or something.

He flashed his best smile, patted me on the leg, and said, "Here we go. Time to dazzle 'em."

Before I could say a word, he was out of the hearse and striding into the building.

I said, "This feels wrong."

Mr. Yunsen cranked the hearse and we pulled away from the building.

"Let him take care of himself. We still have to sell this moonshine."

165

CHAPTER
25

MR. YUNSEN DROVE FASTER, the Buick thundering down the dreary city streets.

"So where does this buyer live?" I asked.

"I have no idea. We're going to his place of business."

A few turns later we were parked behind one of the tallest, glassiest buildings in the city. It must have been five stories high, and I bet from the top you could have seen all the way down into Georgia.

"Give me two minutes," Mr. Yunsen said. He disappeared down a stairway into the bottom of the building.

I slid over into the driver's seat to see if I could figure out how to drive in case I needed to. All the buttons and pedals reminded me of my first ride in the sheriff's automobile. He had operated his vehicle with much less style than Mr. Yunsen, and I decided that I would someday become a champion driver.

A tap on the window startled me, but when I turned, there was Mr. Yunsen, motioning for me.

Mr. Yunsen asked, "You ready to get rid of this shine?"

"More than anything."

At the foot of the stairwell, Mr. Yunsen rapped on a gray metal door. It opened a crack, an eye appearing in the slit and studying us. The door swung open and a seven-hundred-pound gorilla of a man in a suit hustled us in, the door banging shut behind us.

I stood there, motionless, trying to take it all in, but it was too much, like a shotgun blast of sights and sounds. The room was alive with music, except it wasn't the tinny, scratched music from a radio—it was like thunder, and I felt it more than I heard it. Three men with horns gleaming like gold were playing as a short-haired woman in a flowy blue dress like a waterfall crooned into a microphone. It wasn't but mid-morning and these people were partying like it was New Year's Eve.

"How come there are so many people in here?" I asked Mr. Yunsen.

"Graveyard shift at the cotton factory just let out," he said. "For these people, it's midnight."

Inside, it was all tobacco smoke sifting through amber light and the sound of clinking glasses over laughter. Mr. Yunsen guided me up to a long wooden bar with a mirror behind it reflecting countless bottles. A round, smiling man reached over the bar and thrust out a meaty hand.

"Welcome to The Blind Tiger," he yelled over the noise. "I'm Donnie Bridges."

He had the face of a prizefighter, the angles all pushed around and smoothed out. I shook his hand.

"Herbert here tells me that you and I may be able to do some business together." His voice was bright and at the same time briskly professional.

"We may," I answered, as casually as I could.

At this, the man threw back his big bald head and laughed. He turned to Mr. Yunsen and said, "I love it! And people say the American businessman is dead."

Mr. Bridges led us through the crowded room, past women holding thin white cigarettes and men who puffed on cigars the color of melted chocolate. We reached a private booth in the back corner and slid into the black leather seats.

"Okay, now," Mr. Bridges said. "What have you got?"

"Moonshine, sir. Tennessee's finest."

"Tennessee's finest? All right, I'm listening. Who made it?"

"I did, sir."

The smile on the man's face now jumped from ear to ear and he slapped his hands together and laughed.

"Makes the product and sells it too. The kid's going to end the Depression all by himself."

The waitress returned and popped the caps off three bottles of Coca-Cola. I had a big sip. It was ice cold.

"All right, kid. What's your price?" Mr. Bridges asked.

I thought hard for a second. I could tell that Mr. Bridges had a lot of money and he seemed to have taken a liking to me. He seemed like a good guy too, though, and I wasn't there to try to take advantage. I knew exactly what we needed for the farm, and I wouldn't ask for a penny more.

"Seven dollars and fifty cents per gallon. Plus these Coca-Colas, and one for my pa."

"No."

His smile had vanished and something hard crept into his voice.

"No more than five dollars a gallon."

Words did not come to me, and so this rough man and I just looked at each other across the mahogany table. Had I done something wrong? Five dollars a gallon was devastating. Mr. Bridges leaned back, looking very much the owner of his illegal bar.

The giant in the pinstripe suit trudged up to the booth and whispered something in Mr. Bridges's ear. Mr. Yunsen was fidgeting with his bow tie, and I caught him staring at that big bulletproof door we'd come through. It felt like we were sealed into a bank vault. Mr. Yunsen leaned over and said, "It's fine, Cub. The important thing is that we sell it all."

I shook my head and asked him, "Have you got any of our shine on hand?"

Mr. Yunsen reached into his breast pocket and pulled out a slim pewter flask. I took it and slid it across the table.

"Sir."

Mr. Bridges looked down, but didn't touch it.

I said, "As a courtesy."

He reached his beefy hand out and flicked the bottom of the flask. It spun a blur of silver circles then disappeared into his palm. He uncapped it and held it under his nose, then frowned.

"It smells like . . . like . . ."

Holding a finger up to his lips, he tried to place the smell. He cocked his head and stared off into the distance, like the answer was in the cloud of smoke over the bar.

He turned and said, "It smells like . . . Christmas?"

The baffled look on his face only intensified once he took a sip.

"What *is* that?" he asked, licking his lips. With his free hand, he was windmilling his fingers in front of him, trying to churn something out of his memory.

"Sir, it's pumpkin—" I started, but he smacked his palm down on the table.

"Pie!" he cried, his face lighting up. "Pumpkin pie! I knew it! I smelled it and plain as day I was at my Aunt Birdie's on Christmas

Eve with my four brothers, and we're stringing popcorn and cran-
berries on the tree . . ."

"And eating pumpkin pie," I finished for him.

"And eating pumpkin pie," he said, still smiling off into the
memory. "And this is the stuff you're selling?"

"All fifty gallons."

Elbows on the table, Mr. Bridges leaned in conspiratorially and
smiled.

"Look, kid. I'll tell you what I'm going to do. Six bucks a gallon.
And between you and me, I never do six. But this moonshine is
something special. What do you think?"

"I think you must not like Christmas."

Someone kicked me under the table, possibly Mr. Yunsen, but
I ignored him. I was not there to haggle. Seven fifty a gallon, no
more and no less.

I said, "You can keep the Cokes. Seven fifty is firm though."

Mr. Bridges shook his head and said, "You drive a hard bargain,
kid," then stuck his hand across the table for me to shake. "But you
got a deal! I'll take everything you've got."

He whistled between his fingers and the doorman appeared at
the table.

"Go unload the hearse out back. And get the kid another round
of Cokes for the road."

Mr. Yunsen went out with the workers, and me and my new
friend walked around to the back of the bar. This was my first sale.
My first and my last. All these years I'd been busting my hump in
the clearing, and Pa had been having all the fun.

Mr. Bridges glanced around, then pulled a fat wad of green bills
out of his trouser pocket. I couldn't help but smile.

"All right, kid, fifty gallons. And uh, fifty gallons at seven fifty
each, that's . . ."

"Three hundred and seventy-five dollars, sir."

Mr. Bridges shook his head and laughed. "I'm not even surprised anymore, kid. You really are going to save this country," he said as he counted out the bills.

He handed me the money, which I folded into a roll the size of a baseball and stuffed deep into my pocket with my left hand. With my right, I shook Mr. Bridges's hand.

His face grew serious once more, and he said, "Kid, you forget you were ever here, all right?"

I nodded fast as I could. His message was clear as crystal.

As I turned to go, he added, "Unless you need work. Then you come see Mr. Bridges."

"I don't think my teacher would like me working in a bar, sir."

"Maybe not here, but in your area. I've got people who owe me favors all over the state."

"I will keep that in mind, sir."

One of the men who had unloaded the barrels returned with an unopened Coca-Cola bottle and walked me out the metal door and back to the quiet of the city, the music still buzzing in my ears. Mr. Yunsen had turned the Buick around and was waiting for me.

"You sold it all," Mr. Yunsen said as I climbed in.

"I guess that side of the shine business was born into me too."

"You handled yourself remarkably well. I'd never have guessed that was your first time in a speakeasy," Mr. Yunsen said as he edged the hearse back onto the city street.

"What's a speakeasy?" I asked.

"It's a secret club like The Blind Tiger. You're supposed to keep quiet and speak easy so the secret doesn't get out."

"But that was the loudest place I've ever been."

Mr. Yunsen chuckled.

"That's how the best ones are."

"You think my pa did all right?"

Mr. Yunsen said, "I just hope he did half as well as you. We'll know in a few minutes."

CHAPTER
26

As WE PULLED INTO THE parking lot of the Federal Department of Justice, I spotted Pa stretched out on a grassy patch in front of a long line of official-looking black cars. The second I saw him sprawled out there with his pant cuffs nearly up to his knees, bobbing his head to some unheard music, I knew things had gone at least partly well. He was outside and he was free, so that was at least one gamble we'd won.

The brakes on the Buick squeaked as we slowed, and Pa cracked open an eyelid, then popped up and jumped in with us.

"You're all right, Pa," I said, smiling.

"Of course I am."

"And they're going to get Mr. Salvatore?"

"You know what?" he said, biting his lip and smiling. "They are. You were right."

"And you didn't even get in trouble for shining, huh, Pa?"

"They didn't know what to make of me at first. They thought I was trying to trick 'em," Pa said. "Told me they had never seen a shiner come tell 'em where shine was."

I gasped. "They knew you were a shiner?"

"I tried to play it slick, like I had just happened to hear some information. They didn't seem to take me too seriously, and I got to worrying they wouldn't go after Salvatore at all. So I just laid it all out there for them."

"You told 'em we shined," I said.

I couldn't believe it. Pa had confessed.

"Told 'em *I* shined," he corrected. "They had heard about gangs coming out of Chicago and bootlegging. And the Feds will be in Hidden Orchard tomorrow night, looking for Salvatore."

"But what about you?" I asked.

"I made a deal. They won't take me to jail. I've just got to help them in their case against Salvatore. So they catch him, and we'll be fine."

Pa and I were staying together. That was the important thing. And they were going to catch Mr. Salvatore.

"And if they don't catch him?" I asked.

"They'll get him. How'd you do?"

At this, Mr. Yunsen chuckled from behind the wheel. "The casket's empty. You two no longer have any moonshine."

I nodded and said, "I sold it all."

"Well, I'll be," Pa said. "No more shine."

"And I got us free Coca-Colas," I said, holding up a bottle. "I drank one though."

"That's great! Did you get any money?"

"Oh yeah, three hundred and seventy-five dollars."

Pa slapped his knee and said, "Now that is hard to beat."

Mr. Yunsen had packed a lunch of fried chicken and we ate

it cold with salt as the hearse climbed back into the hills toward Hidden Orchard. The Cokes were warm, but still delicious. We ate the chicken and tossed the bones out the window. As we got closer to town, I asked, "So tomorrow we're taking the still to Creamville, right?"

"You got school, Cub."

"What? We've got important work to do. I figured I'd take the rest of the week off."

"We'll load the still early. Then you got to get to school."

"Come on, Pa."

"Nope."

No matter what I said to get out of school, Pa just shook his head. We rode on in silence until the hearse edged up the drive. No other cars were in sight. We arranged to meet with Mr. Yunsen the next morning and then headed out back to bring up the parts of the still.

Lugging the still out of the woods was harder for us than I'd thought it would be, and the two of us cursed our injuries and cursed Mr. Salvatore for causing them. The new flesh on Pa's hands was coming in around the scabs, but it was clear he would always have the scars. And as I tried to grip the big copper kettle, I felt something give way, like a coiled-up spring had popped in my cut hand.

"Agh!" I yelled, thinking one of my fingers had gone flying off.

Bracing myself for the worst, I looked down. There was enough daylight left to see where Mr. Yunsen had sewn me up, the little black tracks marching across my palm. One of the stitches had popped and was flapping loose in the wind.

I broke out laughing and showed Pa.

"It looks like you're holding a caterpillar," he said. "We got a little banged up. But we didn't let anybody stop us."

• • •

175

As day broke, Mr. Yunsen arrived for the final collection. The casket had been removed from the hearse to fit all the pieces of the still. We fought the big kettle for a half hour before the three of us got it up and into the back.

"Just make sure she gets a good home, Herbert," Pa said. "And tell 'em to make sure the drip tube stays clean or it'll foul the taste."

"Sure, Earl."

A whole team of engineers couldn't have built a better still than ours, and Pa had done it himself with nothing but a heap of scrap metal and his own two hands.

Pa turned to me and said, "The still is dead."

"Better it than us," I said.

I slammed the door shut with my good hand.

With the sun hitting the back of my neck, I stared off into the woods, thinking how there was no longer a still, no stockpile of barrels in the tree, no more nights shining. Any trouble we had left would come rumbling into town tonight, and then hopefully be gone for good. I turned and saw Pa was looking in the same direction as me.

"Kind of sad, huh, Pa?"

"Kind of sad I didn't see that I should have done this a long time ago. I'm lucky to have a son like you."

That made me feel real good inside, like me and Pa had both gotten set on a straight course. We walked back in and I grabbed my pencil, a biscuit, and an apple and started to say so long, but Pa was at the door in his coat, waiting for me.

"I'm going to walk with you a while," he said.

"What for?"

"Beats sitting here all day with that gun in my hands."

We headed out, bracing against a strong wind.

I asked, "So the government men are going to get Mr. Salvatore on the road, right? So we probably won't even see him."

"That's what they said. Called it a 'sting' or a 'stinger' or something like that. Said they'd have a couple men in town. So long as they know he's carrying shine, they can arrest him when he's away from the houses and whatnot. In case he goes shooting up the place."

"You think he'd do that?"

"Ain't no telling what a man like that will do."

We walked on down Elm, Pa nodding to people who ignored him back, me lost in my thoughts. Even if we didn't have to see him, just the thought of Mr. Salvatore being in town made me plenty anxious.

"What are we supposed to do then?" I asked.

"Mr. Yunsen said you could wait it out at his place with him and Rebecca. I got to hunker down at the house in case they can't take Salvatore on the road. Feds said for me to make everything natural-looking, light a lantern out front, all that. They'll arrest him the second he turns in the drive. That way they can prove he was going to buy shine and not just passing through town."

I shook my head. "That's a terrible plan."

Pa sighed. "That's the way the law says it's got to be done, and I'll tell you, I feel a bit like a worm on a hook. But I had to make a deal with 'em. And if they don't get Salvatore, well, I ain't got a leg to stand on."

I stopped walking and jerked his sleeve. "It's the part about me going to Mr. Yunsen's that's terrible," I said. "I'm not leaving you at the house alone."

We were standing in front of Beckwith Methodist, and Pa looked at me hard, studying my face.

I said, "I'm staying. You send me to Yunsen's, I'll run right back. You can't stop me."

For a long moment neither one of us spoke. That big clock was ticking in the bell tower up above us, and it felt like we were gunslingers getting ready to draw.

177

"You can't stop me," I repeated.

He finally nodded and said, "I reckon I'm starting to see that. All right then, son," and we kept on walking.

As we neared the schoolhouse, I stopped short and pulled out my pencil.

"I need a note, Pa."

"A note?" he asked, scratching his head. "What for?"

"I don't get it either, Pa. But I need a note from you saying I missed school. They're crazy about notes here."

"Come on, you know I'm no writer. Get your teacher to come out. I'll tell her you had important business yesterday."

I hesitated, wondering if Miss Pounder would tell him I was a bad reader, or that I did foolish things in class. I had enough going on already without embarrassing Pa. But he stood waiting, then motioned to the door with his chin. With a sigh, I headed in, coming back out in the cold with Miss Pounder. She looked at Pa's overalls and long hair and frowned.

"Are you Cub's father?"

Pa gave her a long, dramatic bow and said, "Earl Jennings, at your service."

My mouth fell open an inch and I stood there like I'd taken root in the ground, wondering if Pa was going to kiss her hand or twirl her around or something.

"Yesterday Cub was assisting me with important family matters. He will not be absent again," Pa said. I'd never heard him talk so fancy.

Miss Pounder stood there looking confused, and finally muttered, "Oh, okay. Thank you for telling me."

Inching back toward the schoolhouse, I nodded goodbye to Pa. But as me and Miss Pounder headed in, Pa called, "Make sure you challenge him good. He's real skilled with numbers. Make him as smart as you can."

Miss Pounder looked back and smiled, something I had seen only once or twice in weeks of school, and said, "Of course."

As Miss Pounder and I walked into the classroom, she said, "You're lucky to have a father like that."

CHAPTER
27

WITH **M**R. **S**ALVATORE **COMING** that night to collect, I couldn't even begin to focus on the penmanship lesson at school. Thankfully, Miss Pounder just stood at the chalkboard, drawing lines with her straightedge.

I was copying the sentences when Shane leaned over from his desk.

"Everybody was hoping you'd never come back to school," he whispered.

For a long while, that was exactly what I'd hoped for as well, and yet there I was.

"I don't care," I muttered.

Miss Pounder was still writing on the chalkboard, and Shane leaned over again, leering at me.

"Yesterday we had a party to celebrate you being gone."

I turned away and kept copying the words, but his red hair was flashing in the corner of my eye.

"Rebecca said she was happy you weren't here so she didn't have to babysit you."

I gritted my teeth and leaned toward him.

"Look, you doorknob, I got real problems. I got people after me that would leave you puddling the floor, so you're crackers if you think I'm scared—"

There was a thunderclap in the front of the room and I jumped and saw that Miss Pounder had slammed her yardstick down on her desk. The talking behind her back had set her off something fierce. She glared at the class, her nostrils flaring big as a Clydesdale's. She was showing the first signs of a full-blown conniption fit.

"Who was talking?" she shouted, storming down the aisle, yardstick in hand.

Shane smirked and leaned back in his chair. Out of the corner of my eye, I saw him point a finger toward me.

Miss Pounder was almost upon me. The kindness I'd seen in her outside was a distant memory.

"After-school detention! Plus ten across the hands," she said.

I couldn't stay after school on the most important night of my life. And my hand was already full of stitches. Why couldn't I have just shut up?

"Cub, you hear me?" she said.

From behind me, little Myrtle said, "It wasn't him, Miss Pounder. It was Shane."

My mouth fell open. Myrtle. Sweet Myrtle. Sweet little buck-toothed Myrtle.

From across the room, Russ said, "Shane's been talking all class, Miss Pounder."

Shane's eyes bugged out of his ugly head, and he said, "They're liars. Cub was—"

Rebecca turned and said to him, "He was trying to concentrate,

181

Shane. Some of us are actually smart enough to do the work."

Miss Pounder turned away from me and stuck the yardstick in Shane's face like she was going to bayonet him.

"You, ten after school."

Sitting there on my stump, I looked around at all the other students as they went back to their penmanship. They still thought I was peculiar, I knew that. It would always be like that. I'd grown up too different—they didn't have to work nights or worry about going to jail or burning buckets of gasoline. But if things went okay tonight, I would at least have that in common with them. And even if they didn't particularly care about me one way or the other, they liked Shane a lot less.

Finally free from school, I hurried Rebecca to her turnoff, and she made me promise that tomorrow I'd tell her everything that happened. I half ran down Elm Street, keeping an eye out for any cars, but once I got past Gibbons Drugstore, the energy inside me got to be too much and I flat-out sprinted the rest of the way home.

Rounding the end of our cornfield, I could just make out a figure sitting in a rocker on the porch. The shade coming off the roof made it too dark for me to see who it was, but two steps later I saw the chair rocking so hard it was about to take flight and I knew it was Pa.

"Hey there," Pa said as I ran up the steps. "Have a seat. I got some good news."

I angled my chair so I could see Pa and watch the drive at the same time.

"The still sold," he said. "Two hundred and ten bucks. Yunsen already came by."

We were no longer moonshiners. I felt a lightness in my stomach, like an excitement rising up in me that life was heading into new territory. We now had a chance at good, honest living.

"And you got the money?" I asked.

"Nope," Pa said, still rocking at full speed. "Spent it."

Oh no.

Pa gave the chair one more big rock and used it to shoot himself up to his feet. He reached into the chest pocket of his overalls and pulled out something that twinkled even in the shade.

"Two pieces of brass. One for me and one for you," he said, handing me one of the keys.

"We got it? We got the house?" I asked. I took it and stared, mouth open, like I'd never seen a key in my life.

Pa smiled and put his good hand on my shoulder. "We got it."

So many pictures rushed through my head, images of the pond, of giant tomatoes, of the rich, coffee-colored soil, that I couldn't think straight to talk. I just sat back in my chair, staring at the key in my hand.

The sun finally set behind a thick line of incoming clouds, and me and Pa left the porch and went inside to wait things out. We sat at the table and picked at our beans and rice for a while, but soon took our tin plates into Pa's room so we could watch the window while eating. The shotgun was propped against the wall by Pa's chair.

"You think we'll hear the agents get Mr. Salvatore?" I asked.

"It's only about eight. But if he starts shooting, I bet we'll hear something."

Would Mr. Salvatore try to shoot his way out? Would he come here and shoot his way in?

Pa went out and hung the lamp from a nail on the porch. He came back in and we sat in silence. I watched the clouds as they raced across the sky to blot out the moon, then moved on. Pa now had the Winchester in his lap. All I could hear was the faint whistle of the draft coming from my room. I sat, barely breathing.

Around eleven, a hazy light appeared in the distance. The

yellow glow split into two lights, the headlights of an automobile. The beams swung around the corner and cut across the cornfield like a scythe. I pressed my face to the windowpane.

"Is it the government men?" I asked.

Pa squinted and said, "Can't tell. It looks long though, like Mr. Yunsen's Buick."

It wasn't until the headlights were no longer shining right in my eyes that I got a good look at the vehicle, a large, boxy delivery truck.

"Salvatore," Pa said, his voice shaking.

I looked up at Pa to ask what we should do, but my mouth went dry and I couldn't get any words out. By the look on Pa's face though, he didn't have any answers either. There were no agents there to save us. There was only Mr. Salvatore, speeding toward our house. We both stood stock-still, Pa clenching the shotgun and me staring at him, waiting for him to explain what had happened. The roar of the engine cut off and I didn't hear a thing until a single rap hit the back door like an axe blow.

"Jennings," a voice called. It was definitely Salvatore.

My stomach lurched like I was going to be sick on the floor. Eyes shut, I shook my head. Please just leave us alone.

Salvatore knocked again. I whispered to Pa, "What do we do?"

Pa didn't answer, just picked up the gun and pointed its barrel at the bedroom door as the banging got louder.

I reached over and put my hand on top of the gun barrel, gently pressing it toward the floor. Pa looked at me and I shook my head and whispered, "Don't shoot him, Pa. You'll go to jail. Or the rest of the gang will hunt us down."

Pa shook his head and raised the gun muzzle back up, hand on the pump action.

"Please," I said. "We can get away. We just need to get outside."

Pa stared at me for a long minute, and I wondered if he had any trust left in him. Then he hid the shotgun behind the bedroom door and called, "I'm coming!"

I nodded to him, and together we walked to the back door. As Pa reached for the handle, the door swung open and Mr. Salvatore walked right in. He had his hat pointed low over his eyes.

"What took you so long?" he asked.

"Just trying to get this lamp lit," Pa said, lifting an oil lamp off the counter and fumbling with a match against the wick. "There we go."

He turned the knob and the room brightened, but I still could not see Mr. Salvatore's face.

"Where's the shine?" Salvatore asked.

"It's outside," Pa said.

"No. I shined the headlights into your coop, all around. It's not there."

"Outside in the clearing," I said quickly.

Mr. Salvatore turned and looked down at me, like he was noticing me for the first time.

"Why's it there? You're supposed to be ready."

I answered, "We've got two big fifty-gallon barrels, but me and my pa are banged up and we couldn't get 'em up to the house. If you help us roll 'em then the three of us can load your truck."

Mr. Salvatore said nothing to this, just stared at us in the flickering light of the kerosene lamp.

"You go first," Mr. Salvatore said finally, nodding toward me. "And carry the lamp. And you," he continued, turning toward Pa and pulling his jacket back to expose the butt of a pistol tucked into his pants. "You walk right behind him."

Just a glimpse of the dull metal finish on that revolver made my insides turn cold. We filed out of the house, into the moonlight, me leading the way and Mr. Salvatore pushing us down the trail to the empty clearing.

CHAPTER
28

THE KEROSENE LAMP SWUNG unevenly on its squeaky handle, throwing our shadows wildly across the pines. I walked in front, going slow to gain time to think, and Mr. Salvatore crowded us in from the back. Pa trudged along in the middle, silent.

"Next time have everything ready. And hurry up," said Mr. Salvatore.

Neither me nor Pa spoke, nor did we walk any faster. As we moved down the well-worn path, I kept wondering why the government men had not come. Maybe they hadn't believed Pa after all. Maybe they just didn't care. Now Mr. Salvatore was marching us to an isolated area. The sound of a couple gunshots wouldn't even reach town.

Pa quickened his pace behind me and whispered in my ear, "The tree."

Of course, I realized. Mr. Salvatore knew the trail and the clearing, but he didn't know the rest of the woods. He'd never suspect the tree, much less crawl under the briars on his belly to check if we were hiding in it.

"Meet at the tree. Run straight there," Pa whispered, then slowed back down.

The full moon was bright, almost bright enough to erase the

circle of stars around it. I studied the sky as I walked, boots weaving along the trail by memory. A low line of clouds was blowing in from the east and would soon block out the moonlight for at least a full minute, I reckoned. Might make it dark enough for us to make our escape from Salvatore.

I stopped walking and turned back to face Mr. Salvatore.

"Mister, I don't know if I can load the barrels. My hand hurts real bad now."

Mr. Salvatore crowded in on me and Pa.

"You can cry later. Keep going."

"But it kills," I said, putting my stitched-up palm and the lamp right in Mr. Salvatore's face.

He squinted at the cut, but looked unimpressed.

"So use your other hand. Keep walking. And get that light out of my face."

I did not move the lamp or my hand, just peeked up and saw the edge of the clouds, gray as ash, begin to creep across the face of the moon. If I could blind him with the lamplight, it'd take him a while to get his bearings when it was pitch black. Out of the corner of my eye I saw Pa take a half step toward Mr. Salvatore.

Mr. Salvatore swatted at the lamp. "I said get that light out of my—"

Pa spun and threw both hands into Mr. Salvatore's chest, shoving him to the ground. I heard Salvatore go down, and I took off around the other side, heaving the lantern off to my right. Mr. Salvatore yelled "Hey!" right as the lantern's glass crunched somewhere behind me. With the thick clouds still over the moon, the night was everywhere and the woods were black.

Pa had a straighter shot to the tree, provided he could find his way there off the path. I would have to cut across the trail at some point. I heard breaking branches to my left, followed by the flat patter of shoe soles on the packed dirt of the trail. I cut farther right. There were crashing noises in the brush and a crack like lightning. Gunshot? Impossible. It was too dark for Salvatore to have hit anything more than an arm's length away, and I knew Pa had been running hard. I kept running and soon all I could hear was my own heavy panting.

By the time I reached the edge of the cornfield, the night around me was blessedly silent. Pa had made it safely to the tree after all. He would hole up in there and Salvatore would never know. I just had to get myself safe now.

Mr. Salvatore was probably still on the path, somewhere out there. I ducked into the first row of cornstalks and looked out toward the house. No federal agents, no police had come. The lamp on the porch had burned itself out. Only thing I could see was the giant white truck that said FRISBEE'S PIES in big red letters. It was sitting so low that the bumper almost touched the ground. I knew it must have been packed with shine. Salvatore had probably been driving all over Tennessee collecting barrels to take back North.

I crouched there, catching my breath and trying to figure out what to do. I could creep around the front of the house, make a run for Pa and the tree that way. That had been what Pa had told me to do—go to him.

But how long could we hide in that dark trunk? Maybe one night. We would have to come out sometime, and Mr. Salvatore could come back whenever he wanted and take care of us. If he'd burned Pa for not wanting to shine, what would he do to us now?

Salvatore didn't even have to leave tonight. He could sit in his truck or right at our supper table and wait us out. No one else would come for days. Only possibility would be that Rebecca would see I wasn't at school and come with her grandpa. And then what would Salvatore do to them?

Crouched in the cornstalks, I rubbed my hands together to get warm. My eardrums were throbbing from running in the cold. Me and Pa were all alone out here, just like we'd always been. And if I went to him in the tree, nobody would know what was happening. I needed to get somebody here—Mr. Yunsen, somebody from town, anybody.

I looked at the truck again, its chrome fender shining silver in the moonlight. Maybe I could figure out how to drive it and go get help. But then I remembered all the levers in the sheriff's car and how Mr. Yunsen said you drove almost completely with your feet. Mr. Salvatore would see me fumbling around in his truck and shoot me dead.

An idea started forming in the back of my head. Looking off toward the clearing, I found myself trying to recall what Pa had said when we'd first talked about if moonshine was bad. "Blow you sky-high if it touches flame. Liquid dynamite," he'd said.

A sharp wind rustled through the stalks and I shivered. I was cold. Looking at the pale white-and-silver truck in the moonlight made me colder. A fire would get people here, I thought. A big fire would, at least. And the truck sitting right in front of me probably held a half ton of shine. But if I burned it, would I get blown up? What if I blew up the entire town?

For a solid minute, I looked back and forth between the woods and the truck, thinking, trying to make myself move. The plan had been to go to the tree. Pa had told me that. And the last time I'd broken from his plan, I'd almost gotten him killed. But were we just going to hide there in the woods forever?

I took a deep breath and broke cover, sprinting toward the front porch and bracing for gunshots. I heard only my own boots pounding through the grass.

The house was dark, but I ran straight in the front, sidestepped the table and chairs, and within seconds had grabbed the matches and a few sheets of newspaper from the kitchen. With the can of lamp oil, I slipped right back out the front door.

Peering around the edge of the house, I could see the truck, but I couldn't make out the woods or the trail. My breath was coming in ripples now, jerky breathing, in and out. I would count to three and then run for the truck. One . . . two . . . and the next second I was there, tugging at the passenger door and throwing myself onto the big front seat.

It was almost too dark to see, but as I crawled over the seat into the back, the strong, mediciney smell of shine hit me hard. I ran my fingers around in front of me, finding the curve of an oak barrel. I tried to be careful pouring the kerosene, but it came flooding out, soaking the barrels and my shirtsleeves.

The oil seared into my cut palm as I tried to wipe it from my arms. I set the can down and blew frantically on my hand, then gritted my teeth and picked the can back up. Cry later, I thought. The smell of kerosene had replaced the smell of shine, and I knew I had oil all over me. I dribbled a trail up to the front of the truck, then backed out the passenger door, splashing the front seat as I went. The kerosene can was still about a quarter full, so I lobbed it right onto the driver's seat.

Crouching there behind the passenger door, my hands shook viciously as I struggled to pull the newspaper and matches from my pocket. I crumpled the paper into a ball and set it on the seat. The image of Pa's blackened arms flashed into my head, and the matchbox fell to the grass. The cold, pain, and a strong chokehold of fear had grabbed me, and I wished desperately that I was anywhere but next to that truck, gagging on the fumes. Just light a match, I thought, and my body will do the rest. All I had to do was strike one little match, touch it to the newspaper, then run. I had started thousands of fires. One more big one, and it would be all over.

I fumbled a match out of the box, squeezing it so tightly it nearly snapped. On three, I thought. But on one, my hand had already taken over and lit the match and touched it to the paper. The seat ignited instantly. By two, I was tearing across the grass back to the house. I never got to three because I heard a loud noise right as I reached the porch. It was not the thunderous boom I had expected, but the voice of Mr. Salvatore shouting at me from the edge of the woods.

CHAPTER
29

WITH MY CHEST POUNDING, I ran around the porch, jumped the steps, and stopped at the front door. If Mr. Salvatore came around the front, I would run inside. If I heard him at the back door, I'd make a run for the tree. I didn't hear him coming either way because the next second a roaring explosion ripped the night in half and I was left wondering if I had indeed blown up the whole town. Even with my eyes squeezed tight and my arms clasped over my head, I could feel the flash of fire and the house rattling under my boots.

In the roar, my ears popped, like someone had slapped them and forced air inside my head. On wobbly legs, I slumped against the door. Steadying myself as best I could, I dared to peek around the corner of the house and looked right into a nightmare. Burning chunks of wood rained down into the yard. A white-hot barrel hoop rolled across the scorched grass like a runaway bicycle wheel.

A wall of flames stood where the truck had been, thick orange embers tornadoing up into the wind.

Everything was fire or blackness. I couldn't see Mr. Salvatore. He had either run back into the woods or been blown into the treetops. A rooster crowed from the coop, either thinking daylight had come early or just terrified.

I rubbed my eyes hard and tried to see past the other end of the porch. It was a dark hundred yards to the edge of the woods. Hopefully Pa was in the tree, sitting there safe.

Head down, I took off around the house and made it across the field and into the trees. I didn't slow until I was hugging the giant oak's trunk and feeling my way around to the back side. A voice called, "Cub!" and I spun a circle, but couldn't place where the voice had come from.

"Boy, up here."

Against the orange glow of the sky I saw the silhouette of Pa sitting in the tree.

"You all right?" he said.

"Yeah, Pa. I think so."

"Can you make it up here?"

Ignoring the pain in my hand, I scrambled up the limbs, finally reaching the thick branch Pa was perched on. As I scooted out and sat next to him, I got a good view of the scene below.

There was no truck left, only a pit with flames rising twenty feet into the air. The coop was missing its roof and the chickens were flapping up and over the wall. Our little garden and the back side of the house were both as black as coal. Hopefully the snakes had hightailed it out of there. The house's back door was still standing, but looked so crispy that a breeze would turn it to dust. Our home probably only had ten minutes to live.

Pa said, "I thought you were going to run straight to the tree."

It was pretty obvious I hadn't done what he'd told me to, what with our house turned into a bonfire and all.

"I mean, I was gonna, but . . ."

He chuckled, waving me off.

"But you did something smarter," he said, pointing out past the fire toward town.

A line of dots was coming down the road. Automobiles, at least three of them, approaching to see what had happened. In silence, we sat together and watched the line of lights get closer, finally stopping in front of the house. Men rushed around, scrambling back and forth like ants, finally finding the well and a bucket and throwing water on the fire's edges. They didn't bother with our cabin.

"I'm sorry about the house, Pa."

"Small sacrifice."

"I mean we were moving anyways."

"It's okay. Time to say goodbye."

It was true all we'd really lost was a couple of rotten mattresses, a shotgun, and a table. And we had a new house, a better one. A part of me ached, though, seeing it go up in smoke, remembering all those nights eating supper in there with Pa, laughing. It had been me and him against the world, and that was our fort. But Pa had already been burned once and I'd nearly been blown up just minutes ago, so I figured if there was going to be a burning, better the house than us.

"Any idea where Mr. Salvatore is?" I asked.

Pa lifted my arm and pointed my finger off toward the western field. I pressed my head against my shoulder and looked down my arm like I was sighting in a rifle. Right at the end of my finger, about fifty yards from the blazing crater where the truck had been, was a smoldering black lump.

"No," I gasped. "Did I kill him?"

"Not outright. He's flopped over a time or two since I've been watching him."

He had burned Pa. I had burned him.

"I knew I could right things between us," I said.

Pa turned and frowned at me.

"Wasn't ever anything wrong."

"You know there was, Pa. And I was feeling so danged guilty about you getting hurt."

"You let that guilt of yours fly off in the wind. Maybe we argued a bit, but that's what families do."

"You were just so ornery all the time. I had to make it up to you."

He scoffed.

"Boy, I was the one who got us into this whole mess in the first place. It's not your job to take care of me. You've only got to take care of yourself, and I've seen now you can do it," he said. "The ornery part I can't help you with though."

Whether he wanted to admit it or not, I had put things right between us. Maybe no mending had been needed in his eyes, but on my side I'd had something to prove. To him and to myself.

He said, "You know, I felt like I'd deserted you out there, what with me running off one way, leaving you to run the other."

His voice hitched, and I looked over and saw the firelight reflecting in his eyes.

"Nah, Pa. We had to go separate ways. He couldn't chase the both of us."

"No, he couldn't, and he went after you. He had that .38 trained on the back of your head. Most cowardly thing I've ever seen in my life."

"He was chasing after me?"

I hadn't even realized it. Salvatore could have shot me.

Pa said, "And he's a strong runner for a fat man. I saw him heading toward you, and I turned around and ran right back at

195

him before he could shoot. Jumped on his back and wrapped him up like a spider."

"You jumped on him?"

"I did. We wrestled around there and his pistol went off, but I knew if I held him long enough you'd get away and use your smarts."

"I heard the shot. I was so scared, Pa."

"You don't need to be scared. Not about anything."

For a long moment, we sat high above the growing crowd. People continued to stream in by car, on horseback, and on foot. A pair of long black cars like I'd seen in Knoxville pulled in and I wondered if the agents had finally shown up. Guess we hadn't been that important to them after all. Didn't even bother to show their faces until I'd blown up half the world.

The back wall of the house collapsed inward and I pictured our table and chairs and beds getting crushed into black dust.

"We should go down," I said.

"In a minute," he said, his voice dreamy, like he was falling asleep.

I reckoned tonight had been about as much excitement as any man could desire. I reached over to pat his knee, and he caught my hand in the air without even taking his eyes off the fire. He kept holding it there, and I looked over at him but couldn't make out much besides his grinning face in the firelight. He wore that same contented look I'd always seen when we were working the still and he knew he had the fire at the perfect temperature.

He was so calm, watching our old house turn to nothing but ash and smoke. All our possessions and memories drifting up to the heavens, and him without a care in the world.

Pa swung his boot over so he was straddling the limb and leaning back against the trunk, his hand still clutching mine. Over the top of our hands I could see his shirt, a dark wet stain right under his heart.

"Pa, what's that?" I asked. I tried to lean in and see, but he just kept holding my hand up between us.

Down below, the roof finally caved in and the fire flared up one last time. The firelight illuminated Pa. His shirt was soaked in blood.

"Pa, are you hurt?" I asked, as he slipped his hand out of mine.

He closed his eyes like he was going to sleep, then opened 'em big and smiled at me.

He said, "No sense in us missing each other. You're me and I'm you."

He leaned forward slowly, then tumbled sideways off the limb. I grabbed for him, but he crashed through the briars below and landed on the roots of the tree.

CHAPTER 30

WINTER HAD COME EARLY that year, and my boots crunched across the frosted grass as I made my way to the edge of the woods. The red flannel that was all mine now nearly fit me and I used one sleeve to wipe the dirt off the face of the gravestone. I hadn't been there for months.

"I would have come before, but . . . but things were hard for me for a while, real hard," I said out loud.

My voice came out in a puff of fog that rose and was gone forever. The words echoed in my ears until my cheeks had grown numb. A pair of warblers crossed overhead and chided me, and I rubbed a hand over my face.

"I'll be coming around more now. Can't have you getting lonely."

I heard footsteps coming up the hillside behind me.

"I bet you thought you'd be burying me up here too, didn't you?"

"I knew you were too stubborn," I said over my shoulder.

Pa had slept for four days in the Nashville hospital before waking up. I spent those four days in a chair next to him, eating stale gingerbread and oranges from the Salvation Army and praying as hard as I could. Lucky for him, the bullet had gone through the side of his belly and hadn't torn up his guts too bad. I got Mr. Yunsen to drive up with a lawyer and some special smelling salts, and Pa woke up long enough to sign some papers that meant we gave up the white house. That had been my idea. Pa maybe didn't exactly know what he was signing, but the bank got the white house back, plus they kept a good chunk of the money we'd already paid them. I got the rest of our money back, which I gave right to the doctors who took the bullet out of his belly. It was the finest hospital in the state.

We lost our nice house before we even got to use it, and I didn't care for a second. If Pa had realized I was sacrificing that whole house just for him to get cured, he would have popped up in that hospital bed and lit into me like the devil. I sat there hoping for exactly that.

While Pa was still knocked out, two federal agents came to visit. They didn't even stay long enough to take off their hats. I asked why they hadn't shown up and the tall one told me there had been a whole band of bootleggers around that night and that they got hung up chasing other mobsters. Said they were chasing one another in automobiles, which sounded so ridiculous I figured they were lying. If I hadn't blown up the truck they wouldn't have ever come. Only good thing they did have to say was that Salvatore would be in jail likely 'til he died. Pa had done his duty.

Pa slept for another day, then sat straight up, opened his eyes big as an owl's, and said, "Time to go, boy."

No more than a minute later, he was walking down the hall, and the nurses were all yelling, and patients were gasping at him.

"Thank you for your hospitality," he said. "I just needed a rest and some time to think."

Everybody kept yelling, but he marched straight on like he was leading a parade. I ran up next to him, just grinning.

"Folks here had counted me out, huh?"

"You showed 'em, Pa. You showed 'em good," I said as we walked out that hospital door, me smiling so hard it hurt and him in all his glory, with the back of his hospital gown open.

There on the hill, visiting Ma, we stood shoulder to shoulder.

Flowers were scarce, but I'd brought a handful of yellow goldenrods I'd found under the fence line. I pulled them from under my flannel and set them on her grave. They glowed bright against the pale grass.

Pa said to the gravestone, "Me and the boy here were fixing to move into our old house. That nice white one. He gave it up, though, just to save my sorry hide."

I'd been right enough about Pa's reaction to losing that house. He was beside himself.

I turned to him and said, "Would you have given it up if I'd been the one who'd gotten shot? If you'd needed money to save me?"

He scoffed and looked at me, all indignant. "What do you think?"

I nodded and said, "Well, there you go."

He was quiet, and I thought maybe my words had gotten through to him. It wasn't just about him looking out for me anymore. And as much as Pa liked to complain, things weren't all bad. We'd been staying with the Yunsens the past two months while Pa finished recovering. One cool morning, the two of us had hitched a ride on the back of a hay truck up to the Blind Tiger, where I got to introduce him to Mr. Bridges. The two of them took a liking to each other right off the bat, and when Mr. Bridges told him how popular our pumpkin-pie moonshine was, Pa called me over for a little meeting, which turned out to be our last as shining partners. We decided to pass the secret recipe on to Mr. Bridges. In turn, Mr. Bridges sent a telegram to an old partner near Hidden Orchard who owed him a favor, and not two days later Pa was signed on as a mechanic for some new government project, something rumored to be called the Tennessee Valley Authority. The job was good money and fit Pa's natural talent for fixing things, but meant him being gone months at a time on different projects. A year ago, just the thought of him being gone so long would have killed me dead.

"I'm heading out Saturday," he said. "You sure you'll be all right at Yunsen's?"

"Sure, Pa. And I'll see you for Christmas."

"You can count on that. And really when you think about it, it ain't long at all 'til then. I'll be back before you know it. Shoot, you just blink your eyes and I'll be right back here."

I wondered if he was talking more for me or for himself.

"You know, Pa, I finally got to understanding the last thing you said to me. Right before you fell out of the tree. You remember what you said?"

We were both still staring at her grave, but I heard him chuckle and he said, "'No sense in us missing each other. You're me and I'm you.'"

"I get it now. It's like as long as I'm living, you're living too. That's what family means," I said. "That's nice. Almost poetic."

"Thank you."

The wind whistled over the crowns of the eastern pines and I could feel a stinging in the tops of my ears.

"Who'd you steal it from?" I asked.

He laughed and nodded toward the ground before us.

"Your ma. Those were her last words to me."